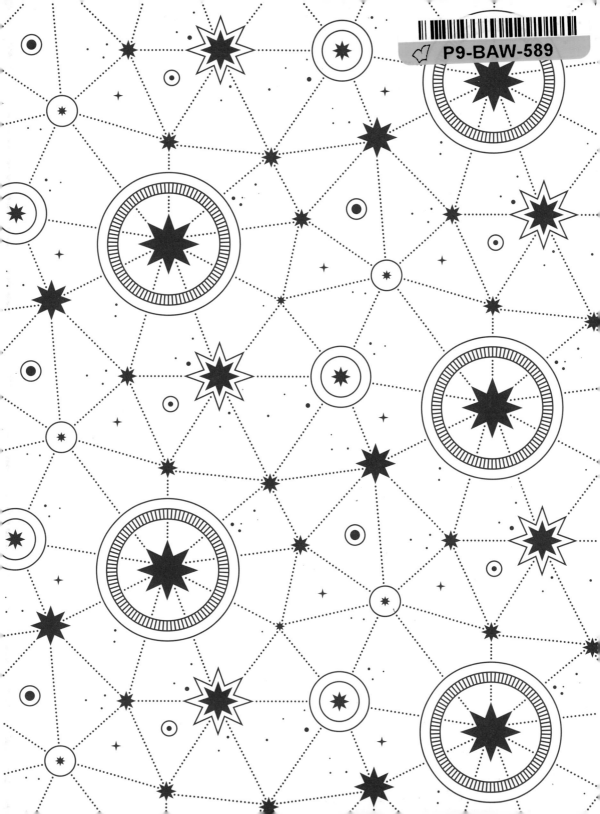

THE UNOFFICIAL

ULTIMATE

HARRY POTTER

SPELLBOOK

A COMPLETE GUIDE TO
EVERY SPELL IN THE WIZARDING WORLD

TABLE OF
CONTENTS

A Word on Spellcasting

Though witches and wizards do not necessarily need wands to perform magic (more on this on the following page), they are considered extremely useful tools in focusing one's abilities. For the best results, use a wand that you have won, inherited or, if selecting a new wand, one which "chooses" you. Practice dueling is not recognized as a way of winning another wizard's wand, as the wand senses the situation is not significant. It should also be noted that, with the exception of the Elder Wand, a wand won from its original master will perform well for the new owner, but will likely retain some allegiance to its old owner.

> **NOTES** You can use any instrument to channel your magic, but using another wizard's wand that you have not won may lead to noticeable discomfort when spellcasting.

Tread with caution when using a broken wand, as it is an unpredictable vessel through which to perform magic. It cannot be recommended for use unless professionally repaired.

Spellotape is definitely not considered a "professional repair."

Nonverbal & Wandless Spells

Nonverbal and wandless spells are extremely difficult to master, though most underage wizards are capable of producing magic in times of great stress. Students at Hogwarts begin learning nonverbal spells in their sixth year, while wandless spellcasting is usually only done by the most skilled witches and wizards, or more commonly in cultures which traditionally practice wandless magic.

MAGIC MOMENT In *Order of the Phoenix*, Harry Potter is able to cast the Lumos spell in a dark alley where he had dropped his wand, enabling him to find it again. This is a good example of a strong connection between a wand and its owner.

Wand Woods

Together with its core and master, the wood a wand is made from influences its characteristics and temperament. Only a small percentage of trees are suitable for wand-making.

Bowtruckle never nest in ordinary trees.

ACACIA Produces selective wands that only work for their owner.

ALDER Pairs well with agreeable witches and wizards.

APPLE Powerful wood, though unsuitable for Dark magic.

ASH Highly loyal; will not perform well for anyone but its true owner.

Ron's first wand—originally Charlie's.

ASPEN Performs martial magic well; often used by duelists.

BEECH A poor match for those who are close-minded.

BLACKTHORN Performs well for fighters; becomes better bonded to its owner after being used in a dangerous situation.

BLACK WALNUT Pairs well with a mindful owner; can be exceptionally useful for charmwork.

CEDAR Often chooses particularly shrewd witches and wizards.

CHERRY Very rare and often makes for a wand with destructive power.

CHESTNUT Often favored by witches and wizards who work with magical beasts and Herbology.

CYPRESS Pairs well with those who are gallant and unselfish.

Remus's wand.

DOGWOOD Makes for peculiar wands that refuse to perform nonverbal spells.

EBONY Excellent for dueling and Transfiguration, especially among those who are self-assured.

ELDER Elder wands are the most rare and are notoriously difficult to master. They often choose remarkable masters.

ELM Prefers dignified owners and is known for producing refined charms and spells with few accidents or errors.

ENGLISH OAK Produces extremely loyal wands that prefer equally loyal owners.

FIR Excellent for use in Transfiguration; prefers a decisive and confident owner.

HAWTHORN Well-suited for both curses and healing magic.

HAZEL Not recommended for those who can't control their temper; is the only wand wood that naturally detects water underground.

HOLLY Well-suited for those prone to emotional outbursts; often selects a master who must undergo a perilous quest.

Harry's wand

HORNBEAM Mates for life with its owner; often chooses passionate owners with a singular vision.

LARCH Known for making its owner more self-assured.

LAUREL A poor match for an apathetic owner; known to perform powerfully for an owner seeking glory.

MAPLE Well suited to determined owners who enjoy travel.

PEAR One of the most resilient woods, often chooses sage and benevolent owners.

PINE Well suited to nonverbal spells; always selects an individualistic owner.

POPLAR Consistently performs well; chooses an owner with distinct principles.

RED OAK Pairs well with an owner possessing quick reflexes; makes for an excellent dueling wand.

REDWOOD Reputed to be good luck; in fact, these wands have a knack for choosing owners who are predisposed to making smart choices.

ROWAN Produces especially strong defensive charms; chooses witches and wizards with a strong sense of morals.

SILVER LIME Favored for its unusual color and rumored to be especially useful for Seers and Legilimens.

SPRUCE Not recommended for hesitant witches or wizards; performs best for self-assured spell-casters with a good sense of humor.

SYCAMORE Pairs well with those looking for adventure; will become bored with mundane requests from its owner.

VINE Often chooses owners who wish to accomplish something out of the ordinary.

Hermione's wand.

WALNUT Commonly pairs well with owners of superior intelligence; makes for a dangerous weapon if the owner lacks morals.

WILLOW Carries the power of healing; often chooses owners who are unsure of themselves in some way.

Ron's second wand.

YEW Reputed to be particularly fearsome dueling wands; often chooses both heroes and villains.

Voldemort's wand.

NOTES ON LENGTH & FLEXIBILITY

LENGTH Most wands measure between 9 and 14 inches, with longer wands being drawn to those with lively personalities and a tendency for the dramatic. By contrast, shorter wands generally choose witches and wizards who wish to produce more refined magic. Wands that measure 8 inches or less are known to choose those who are "short" on character.

FLEXIBILITY A wand's flexibility is usually an indicator of its (and its chosen owner's) own adaptability. However, as with all aspects of wand-making and ownership, this is just one factor among core, wood type, length and the owner's personality and experience, all of which combine to make each wand distinct from any other.

Supreme Wand Cores

Wandmakers around the world will use a wide variety of magical substances for the cores of wands, but Garrick Ollivander will only create wands made with unicorn hair, dragon heartstring or phoenix feathers.

UNICORN HAIR Known for creating reliable wands that rarely experience blockages. Extremely loyal and moralistic, these wands are exceptionally difficult to use when practicing Dark Arts. Unicorn hair may also produce less powerful magic than other substances, and can "die" and need replacing if not properly handled.

DRAGON HEARTSTRING Unsurprisingly, a wand with a core from such a powerful creature also produces the most powerful forms of magic. Another advantage is its ability to learn quickly and bond well with its owner (even a new one). However, it should also be known that dragon heartstring is the most temperamental of the three Supreme Wand Cores and therefore most likely to produce accidents.

PHOENIX FEATHER Phoenix feathers are the rarest type of wand core. They have the ability to produce the greatest range of magic and are known to act of their own accord, a trait that many witches and wizards are not fond of. Phoenix core wands are also known to be the most finicky when choosing their wizard and can be difficult to master.

Other known wand cores: Veela hair, thestral hair, troll whisker, Horned Serpent horn, Basilisk horn.

CHAPTER 1

SPELLS

All known counter spells, healing spells, transfiguration spells and otherwise uncategorized spells in the Wizarding World.

transfiguration changes an object's function, or what it is.

Anapneo

TYPE Healing Spell

PRONUNCIATION Ah-nap-nee-oh

USE Clears a blocked throat

ETYMOLOGY In Greek, *anapneo* means "I breathe."

MAGIC MOMENT In *Half-Blood Prince*, Slughorn uses this spell on a student who has begun to choke on his food.

NOTES This spell may be used in any situation that would otherwise require the Heimlich maneuver.

Apparate

TYPE Teleportation Spell

PRONUNCIATION N/A

USE To teleport oneself to another place

ETYMOLOGY In Latin, *appareo* means "to become visible or appear."

MAGIC MOMENT In *Half-Blood Prince*, Harry and the other sixth-years are able to take Apparition classes. They must learn the three D's: destination, determination and deliberation.

PREFERRED MOVEMENT Turn on the spot

NOTES Witches and wizards must be 17 years old to take their Apparition Test. Underage wizards may travel by Side-Along Apparition.

Watch out for splinching!

Arania Exumai

TYPE Spell

PRONUNCIATION *Ah-rain-ee-ah ex-ooh-may*

USE To blast or repel spiders

ETYMOLOGY In Latin, *aranea* means "spider," while *exumai* may derive from *exuo* ("refuse") or *eximo* ("banish").

MAGIC MOMENT In the *Chamber of Secrets* film, Harry uses this spell to save himself and Ron from the Acromantulas in the Forbidden Forest.

NOTES The light produced by Arania Exumai is presumably very hot, as evidenced by scorch marks left by a narrowly missed spell.

Arrow-Shooting Spell

TYPE Conjuration

PRONUNCIATION Unknown

USE To produce arrows from one's wand

ETYMOLOGY N/A

MAGIC MOMENT Fans of the Appleby Arrows would use this spell in support of the Quidditch team until it was outlawed when a referee was hit by a stray arrow.

NOTES The only known reference to this spell is in *Quidditch Through the Ages*.

Avifors

TYPE Transfiguration

PRONUNCIATION *Ah-vih-fors*

USE Transforms target into bird, flock of birds or (occasionally) flock of bats

ETYMOLOGY In Latin, *avis* means "bird" and *forma* means "shape."

MAGIC MOMENT Minerva McGonagall teaches this spell in first- and second-year Transfiguration classes.

NOTES This spell is only mentioned in some *Harry Potter* video games and the *Harry Potter Trading Card Game*.

Avis

TYPE Conjuration

PRONUNCIATION *Ah-viss*

USE To conjure birds

ETYMOLOGY In Latin, *avis* means "bird."

PREFERRED MOVEMENT

MAGIC MOMENT Garrick Ollivander used this spell to test the wands of the champions in the 1994 Triwizard Tournament.

NOTES When this spell is performed, the caster's wand will smoke and make a loud bang.

Brackium Emendo

TYPE Healing Spell

PRONUNCIATION
Br-ah-key-um eh-men-doh

USE To heal broken bones

ETYMOLOGY In Latin, *bracchium* means "arm" and *emendo* means "mend."

MAGIC MOMENT Gilderoy Lockhart uses this spell improperly on Harry Potter, resulting in his arm bones vanishing instead of healing.

NOTES This may or may not be a legitimate healing spell.

Bubble-Producing Spell

TYPE Conjuration

PRONUNCIATION Unknown

USE To create long-lasting bubbles

ETYMOLOGY N/A

MAGIC MOMENT Filius Flitwick used this spell to decorate the Great Hall's Christmas tree in *Sorcerer's Stone.*

NOTES Ron's wand also produced bubbles while it was broken, but it is unlikely this spell was the cause.

Cauldron to Sieve

TYPE Transfiguration

PRONUNCIATION Unknown

USE Turn a cauldron into a sieve

ETYMOLOGY N/A

MAGIC MOMENT N/A

> NOTES This spell is only referenced in the *Harry Potter Trading Card Game*.

Cribbing Spell

TYPE Spell

PRONUNCIATION Unknown

USE Helps the caster cheat on exams

ETYMOLOGY N/A

MAGIC MOMENT In the *Philosopher's Stone* video game, a Slytherin student asks, "Know any good cribbing spells?"

> NOTES This spell is only mentioned in the *Philosopher's Stone* video game.

Crinus Muto

TYPE Transfiguration

PRONUNCIATION *Cree-nuss mew-toe*

USE Change color and style of the caster's hair

ETYMOLOGY In Latin, *crinis* means "hair" and *muto* means "to change."

MAGIC MOMENT In *Half-Blood Prince*, Ron winds up giving himself a fine handlebar mustache while attempting to learn this spell in Transfiguration class.

NOTES In *LEGO Harry Potter: Years 5–7*, this spell is used to change hair color and style.

Draconifors

TYPE Transfiguration

PRONUNCIATION *Drah-con-ih-fors*

USE Turns small objects into dragons

ETYMOLOGY In Latin, *draco* means "dragon" and *forma* means "shape."

MAGIC MOMENT Minerva McGonagall teaches this spell in third-year Transfiguration class.

NOTES This spell is only seen in the *Prisoner of Azkaban* video game.

Produces much smaller, less powerful creatures than true dragons.

Ears to Kumquats

TYPE Transfiguration

PRONUNCIATION Unknown

USE Turns target's ears into kumquats

ETYMOLOGY N/A

MAGIC MOMENT Harry and Ron learn about this spell when they meet Luna Lovegood for the first time in *Order of the Phoenix.*

NOTES According to a 1995 issue of *The Quibbler*, the spell would be revealed if a reader read the runes it featured upside down.

Episkey

TYPE Healing Spell

PRONUNCIATION *Eh-pihs-key*

USE To heal minor injuries

ETYMOLOGY In Greek, *episkevi* means "repair."

MAGIC MOMENT In *Half-Blood Prince,* Nymphadora Tonks uses this spell to heal Harry's broken nose after his run-in with Draco on the Hogwarts Express.

NOTES In the film version of *Half-Blood Prince,* it is Luna Lovegood who finds Harry on the train and heals him with this spell.

Epoximise

TYPE Transfiguration

PRONUNCIATION *Ee-pox-ih-myse*

USE To bond two objects together

ETYMOLOGY In English, *epoxy* is a type of adhesive.

MAGIC MOMENT In the *Fantastic Beasts and Where to Find Them* film, an issue of the magazine *Transfiguration Today* touts a debate on "the pros and cons of epoximising."

NOTES This spell is first referenced in the *Harry Potter Trading Card Game*.

Evanesce

TYPE Transfiguration

PRONUNCIATION *Eh-van-ess*

USE To make objects disappear

ETYMOLOGY In English, *evanesce* means "to pass out of sight, memory or existence."

MAGIC MOMENT In the *Harry Potter Trading Card Game*, this spell's card quotes *Chamber of Secrets*: "Professor McGonagall's classes were always hard work, but today was especially difficult."

NOTES This spell is very similar to the more commonly referenced Evanesco.

Evanesco

TYPE Transfiguration

PRONUNCIATION Eh-van-ess-co

USE To vanish objects

ETYMOLOGY In Latin, *evanesco* means "I vanish."

MAGIC MOMENT In *Order of the Phoenix*, this spell is taught to Hogwarts students in their fifth year. Minerva McGonagall introduced the spell by having the students practice vanishing snails and other small creatures, a task at which only Hermione excelled.

> **NOTES** As Minerva McGonagall explains, vanished objects go "into non-being, which is to say, everything."

Objects can be enchanted to resist vanishing spells—the Weasley twins took advantage of that when designing their fireworks.

Everte Statum

TYPE Spell

PRONUNCIATION Ee-ver-tay stah-tum

USE To make an opponent stumble backward; also causes temporary sharp pain

ETYMOLOGY In Latin, *everte* means "to throw out" and *statum* means "stand."

MAGIC MOMENT In the *Chamber of Secrets* film, Draco Malfoy uses this spell on Harry during Dueling Club.

> **NOTES** The strength of the spell will determine how much pain the target experiences. The spell does not cause lasting damage.

Extinguishing Spell

TYPE Spell

PRONUNCIATION Unknown

USE To put out fires

ETYMOLOGY N/A

MAGIC MOMENT In *Goblet of Fire*, Charlie Weasley mentions he and the other dragon keepers would perform extinguishing spells if something went wrong during the first task of the Triwizard Tournament.

> **NOTES** This spell may be the same as Aqua Eructo.

Eye of Rabbit, Harp String Hum, Turn this Water into Rum

TYPE Transfiguration

PRONUNCIATION As written

USE To turn water into rum

ETYMOLOGY N/A

MAGIC MOMENT In the *Sorcerer's Stone* film, Seamus Finnigan attempts to use this spell. He only manages to produce weak tea before causing an explosion.

> **NOTES** Like "Sunshine, daisies, butter mellow, turn this stupid, fat rat yellow," this spell does not follow the normal convention of other spell names and may not be a real spell.

Ferula

TYPE Healing Spell

PRONUNCIATION *Fer-oo-la*

USE To bandage and splint broken bones

ETYMOLOGY In Latin, *ferula* means "rod."

MAGIC MOMENT In *Prisoner of Azkaban*, Remus Lupin uses this spell to splint Ron's broken leg.

NOTES This spell may also be classified as a Conjuration.

Finite

TYPE Counter-spell

PRONUNCIATION *Fin-ee-tay*

USE Terminates another spell's effects

ETYMOLOGY In Latin, *finite* means "to end."

MAGIC MOMENT In *Deathly Hallows*, Harry shouts "Finite!" to steady a rampart that Vincent Crabbe had tried to knock down using Descendo.

NOTES It is unclear whether this spell is less powerful or otherwise different from Finite Incantatem.

Finite Incantatem

TYPE Counter-spell

PRONUNCIATION *Fin-ee-tay in-can-tah-tem*

USE Terminates another spell's effects

ETYMOLOGY In Latin, *finite* means "to end" and *incanto* means "having been bewitched."

MAGIC MOMENT In *Deathly Hallows*, Hermione suggests Ron use the spell to stop the rain falling in Yaxley's office.

NOTES This counter-spell may not be effective against Dark spells, which can require specific counter-curses.

Firestorm

TYPE Conjuration

PRONUNCIATION Unknown

USE To produce a large ring of fire

ETYMOLOGY N/A

MAGIC MOMENT In *Half-Blood Prince*, Albus Dumbledore casts this spell to protect himself and Harry from Inferi, which had been guarding the hiding spot of one of Voldemort's Horcruxes.

NOTES This spell may produce everlasting Gubraithian Fire, as evidenced by the fact that the cave's water did not extinguish it.

Flagrate

TYPE Conjuration

PRONUNCIATION Flah-grah-tay

USE To create lines of fire which can be used to write or draw in the air

ETYMOLOGY In Latin, *flagro* means "blaze" or "glowing."

MAGIC MOMENT In *Order of the Phoenix*, Hermione uses this spell to draw X's on doors in the Ministry of Magic's Department of Mysteries.

NOTES The lines of fire created with this spell will remain for some time.

Fumos

TYPE Conjuration

PRONUNCIATION Fyoo-mohs

USE To create a defensive cloud of smoke (aka Smokescreen Spell)

ETYMOLOGY In Latin, *fumo* means "smoke."

PREFERRED MOVEMENT

MAGIC MOMENT This spell is taught in Professor Quentin Trimble's book, *The Dark Forces: A Guide to Self-Protection*.

NOTES This spell is seen in the *Harry Potter Trading Card Game* and the *Chamber of Secrets* and *Prisoner of Azkaban* video games. In the video games, Fumos Duo is a more powerful version of this spell.

Herbifors

TYPE Transfiguration

PRONUNCIATION *Erhb-ih-fors*

USE Turns target's hair into flowers

ETYMOLOGY From the English *herb*, referring to plants, and the Latin *forma*, meaning "shape."

MAGIC MOMENT This spell can be purchased at Wiseacre's Wizarding Equipment in Diagon Alley.

NOTES This spell is only seen in the *LEGO Harry Potter* video games.

Homenum Revelio

TYPE Spell

PRONUNCIATION *Hoh-min-nuhm ruh-vay-lee-oh*

USE To reveal human presence

ETYMOLOGY In Latin, *hominem* means "humans," and *revelo* means "I reveal."

MAGIC MOMENT In *Deathly Hallows*, Hermione used this spell to make sure there weren't any Death Eaters at 12 Grimmauld Place.

NOTES According to J.K. Rowling, Albus Dumbledore was able to detect Harry's presence under his Invisibility Cloak with a nonverbal version of this spell.

Hot-Air Spell

TYPE Conjuration

PRONUNCIATION Unknown

USE To conjure a stream of hot air from the tip of a caster's wand

ETYMOLOGY N/A

MAGIC MOMENT In *Order of the Phoenix*, Hermione uses this spell to dry her snow-covered robes.

NOTES Hermione performed this spell by doing a "complicated little wave" with her wand.

Inanimatus Conjurus

TYPE Transfiguration

PRONUNCIATION In-ahn-ih-may-tus con-jur-us

USE To conjure inanimate objects (presumably)

ETYMOLOGY From the English words *inanimate* and *conjure*.

MAGIC MOMENT In *Order of the Phoenix*, Minerva McGonagall assigned an essay on this spell.

NOTES McGonagall likely assigned this essay to prepare her students for learning about Conjuring Spells.

Incarcerous

TYPE Conjuration

PRONUNCIATION In-kar-cer-us

USE To conjure ropes that bind the target

ETYMOLOGY In Latin, *incarcerus* means "to jail" or "to imprison."

MAGIC MOMENT In *Half-Blood Prince*, Harry attempts to use this spell against the attacking Inferi. Though it worked on its targets, there were too many Inferi for it to be effective overall.

NOTES The ropes may also be used to strangle a target, as seen in the film version of *Order of the Phoenix* when Dolores Umbridge uses this spell on a centaur named Magorian.

Incendio

Always check to see if Muggles have blocked their chimneys.

TYPE Conjuration

PRONUNCIATION In-sen-dee-oh

USE To conjure fire

ETYMOLOGY In Latin, *incendium* means "fire."

MAGIC MOMENT In *Goblet of Fire*, Arthur Weasley uses this spell to light the Dursleys' fireplace so that he, his sons and Harry may travel by Floo powder.

NOTES In *Harry Potter* video games, Incendio Duo and Incendio Tria are more powerful versions of this spell.

Lacarnum Inflamari

TYPE Conjuration

PRONUNCIATION *La-kar-num in-fla-mar-ree*

USE To set a cloak on fire

ETYMOLOGY In Latin, *lacerna* means "cloak" and *inflammare* means "to ignite."

MAGIC MOMENT In the film version of *Sorcerer's Stone*, Hermione uses this spell to set Severus Snape's cloak on fire, believing him to be jinxing Harry's Nimbus 2000.

NOTES In the book, Hermione used Bluebell Flames to light Snape's cloak on fire.

Lapifors

TYPE Transfiguration

PRONUNCIATION *Lap-ih-fors*

USE To turn a target into a rabbit

ETYMOLOGY In Latin, *lepus* means "hare" and *forma* means "shape."

MAGIC MOMENT Minerva McGonagall teaches this spell to her third-year students.

NOTES When successfully performed, the caster can control the newly Transfigured rabbit's movements. This spell is only mentioned in the *Harry Potter* video games and the *Harry Potter Trading Card Game*.

Legilimens

TYPE Spell

PRONUNCIATION Le-jill-ih-mens

USE To delve into a target's mind

ETYMOLOGY In Latin, *legere* means "to read" and *mens* means "mind."

MAGIC MOMENT In *Order of the Phoenix*, Severus Snape uses this spell on Harry multiple times while trying to teach him Occlumency. Snape presumably also used this spell nonverbally many times before, as suggested by Harry's feeling that Snape could read minds.

NOTES Highly skilled Legilimens can implant false visions into a person's mind, as shown in *Order of the Phoenix* when Voldemort tricks Harry into believing his godfather, Sirius Black, is in danger at the Department of Mysteries.

Liberacorpus

TYPE Counter-spell

PRONUNCIATION Lib-er-ah-kor-pus

USE To counteract Levicorpus, resulting in a target's body no longer being suspended in the air

ETYMOLOGY In Latin, *liberare* means "to free" and *corpus* means "body."

MAGIC MOMENT In *Half-Blood Prince*, Harry uses this spell on Ron after he had tested out Levicorpus, which hoisted Ron in the air by the ankle.

NOTES Both this spell and its counterpart, Levicorpus, were invented by Severus Snape.

Morsmordre

TYPE Conjuration

PRONUNCIATION *Morz-more-druh*

USE To conjure the Dark Mark

ETYMOLOGY In French, *mort* means "death" and *mordre* means "to bite."

MAGIC MOMENT In *Goblet of Fire*, Barty Crouch Jr. casts this spell after the Quidditch World Cup with the aim of scaring former Death Eaters who were rioting and torturing Muggles at the event.

NOTES During the First Wizarding War, Death Eaters often cast this spell after having committed a murder.

Multicorfors

TYPE Transfiguration

PRONUNCIATION *Mull-tee-core-fors*

USE To change the color and style of a target's clothing

ETYMOLOGY In Latin, *multus* means "many" and *forma* means "shape," while *cor* is likely derived from "color."

MAGIC MOMENT In the *LEGO Harry Potter* video games, this spell can be purchased at The Leaky Cauldron.

NOTES This spell is only mentioned in the *LEGO Harry Potter* video games.

Obscuro

TYPE Conjuration

PRONUNCIATION Ob-skur-oh

USE To conjure a blindfold, obscuring a target's vision

ETYMOLOGY In Latin, *obscuro* means "dark" or "concealed."

MAGIC MOMENT In *Deathly Hallows*, Hermione uses this spell on the portrait of Phineas Nigellus Black in an attempt to keep him from learning their location.

NOTES This spell is mentioned once more in the *Harry Potter* universe, when Harry uses it on Draco Malfoy while dueling with him in *Cursed Child*.

Orchideous

TYPE Conjuration

PRONUNCIATION Or-kid-ee-us

USE To conjure flowers

ETYMOLOGY In Latin, *Orchideae* is the name for the orchid plant family.

MAGIC MOMENT In *Goblet of Fire*, Garrick Ollivander uses this spell to test Fleur Delacour's wand during the Weighing of the Wands ceremony.

NOTES In the *Goblet of Fire* video game, Orchideous is the incantation for a jinx that turns a target into a flowering shrub.

Periculum

TYPE Conjuration

PRONUNCIATION *Puh-rick-you-lum*

USE To conjure red sparks

ETYMOLOGY In Latin, *periculum* means "danger."

MAGIC MOMENT In the *Goblet of Fire* film, Harry uses this spell to send up red sparks during the third task when Fleur Delacour is being dragged into the maze.

NOTES This spell may be an alternate version of Red Sparks.

Point Me

TYPE Spell

PRONUNCIATION As written

USE To use wand as a compass

ETYMOLOGY N/A

MAGIC MOMENT In *Goblet of Fire*, Hermione teaches this spell to Harry so he can navigate the third task of the Triwizard Tournament: a giant maze.

NOTES This spell is rare for having an incantation that is in English rather than Latin.

Purple Firecrackers

TYPE Conjuration

PRONUNCIATION Unknown

USE To conjure purple firecrackers

ETYMOLOGY N/A

MAGIC MOMENT In *Sorcerer's Stone*, Albus Dumbledore uses this spell to quiet the Great Hall after Quirinus Quirrell announces there is a troll in the school dungeons.

NOTES This spell is also used in the *Harry Potter Trading Card Game*.

Reparifors

TYPE Healing spell

PRONUNCIATION *Re-par-ih-fors*

USE To heal ailments such as poisoning or paralysis

ETYMOLOGY Likely from the English *repair* and the Latin *forma*, meaning "shape."

MAGIC MOMENT In the *Prisoner of Azkaban* video game, this spell is cast using Chocolate Frog Card combinations.

NOTES This spell is only mentioned in the *Prisoner of Azkaban* video game.

Reparifarge

TYPE Untransfiguration

PRONUNCIATION *Reh-par-ih-fahj*

USE To reverse the Transfiguration of an object

ETYMOLOGY In Latin, *reparo* means "repair" and *forma* means "shape."

MAGIC MOMENT Minerva McGonagall teaches this spell to second-year students in her Transfiguration class.

NOTES This spell is only mentioned in the video game *Harry Potter: Hogwarts Mystery.*

Revelio

TYPE Untransfiguration

PRONUNCIATION *Reh-vel-ee-oh*

USE To reveal a person or object's true appearance and make the invisible visible

ETYMOLOGY In Latin, *revelo* means "unveil" or "uncover."

MAGIC MOMENT In the *Fantastic Beasts and Where to Find Them* film, Newt Scamander uses this spell on Percival Graves, revealing he is actually Gellert Grindelwald.

NOTES This spell can also be used to reveal messages and passages.

Rose Growth

TYPE Transfiguration

PRONUNCIATION Unknown

USE To accelerate the growth of a rosebush

ETYMOLOGY N/A

MAGIC MOMENT This spell is used in the *Harry Potter Trading Card Game*.

NOTES Rose Growth may be related to Herbivicus.

Serpensortia

TYPE Conjuration

PRONUNCIATION *Ser-pen-sore-tee-ah*

USE To conjure a snake

ETYMOLOGY In Latin, *serpens* means "serpent" and *ortus* means "created."

MAGIC MOMENT In *Chamber of Secrets*, Draco Malfoy uses this spell while sparring with Harry during the first Dueling Club meeting.

NOTES According to the official Warner Bros. *Harry Potter* website, this "snake summons" spell was invented in India and is (illegally) used by those whom Muggles call "snake charmers."

Shield Penetration Spell

TYPE Conjuration

PRONUNCIATION Unknown

USE To dismantle magical shields

ETYMOLOGY N/A

MAGIC MOMENT In *Deathly Hallows: Part 2*, Voldemort uses this spell to overpower the defensive enchantments placed over Hogwarts Castle.

NOTES The Elder Wand cracks when Voldemort uses this spell, implying it took an incredible amount of power to break through such strong shields.

Might have been more difficult because he was not the wand's master.

Shooting Spell

TYPE Spell

PRONUNCIATION Unknown

USE To shoot a target, similar to a gun

ETYMOLOGY N/A

MAGIC MOMENT In a deleted scene from *Deathly Hallows: Part 1*, Harry and Ron use this spell to attempt to catch a rabbit while camping in the forest.

NOTES This spell produces a sound like a gunshot.

Smashing Spell

TYPE Spell

PRONUNCIATION Unknown

USE To create an explosion to destroy a target

ETYMOLOGY N/A

MAGIC MOMENT In the *Half-Blood Prince* film, Bellatrix Lestrange celebrates Albus Dumbledore's death by using this spell to smash windows in the Great Hall.

NOTES This spell may be the same as the Reductor Curse.

Stealth Sensoring Spell

TYPE Spell

PRONUNCIATION Unknown

USE To detect the presence of those under magical disguise

ETYMOLOGY N/A

MAGIC MOMENT Dolores Umbridge had spells of this nature placed around entrances to her office after Lee Jordan had levitated Nifflers in through her window.

NOTES This spell is only mentioned in *Order of the Phoenix*.

Switching Spell

TYPE Transfiguration

PRONUNCIATION Unknown

USE To switch the placement of two objects

ETYMOLOGY N/A

PREFERRED MOVEMENT

MAGIC MOMENT Hermione mused about Harry using this spell to switch the dragon's teeth for wine gums in the first task of the Triwizard Tournament, but realized it was unlikely to be effective, as dragonhide is particularly difficult for spells to penetrate.

> **NOTES** According to Minerva McGonagall, this spell is very simple, though in *Goblet of Fire*, Neville Longbottom has particular difficulty with it and somehow manages to place his own ears on a cactus.

Teleportation Spell

TYPE Spell

PRONUNCIATION Unknown

USE To instantly transport objects from one place to another

ETYMOLOGY N/A

MAGIC MOMENT In *Half-Blood Prince*, Albus Dumbledore uses this spell to send Harry's belongings ahead to the Burrow so they can visit Horace Slughorn unencumbered.

> **NOTES** Vanishing Cabinets may be enchanted with this spell.

Unbreakable Vow

TYPE Spell

PRONUNCIATION Unknown

USE To make a magically binding oath

ETYMOLOGY N/A

MAGIC MOMENT As children, Fred and George Weasley once tried to make an Unbreakable Vow with Ron. This enraged their normally calm father, Arthur Weasley, as the effect of breaking an Unbreakable Vow is death. Allegedly, Fred's left buttock has never been the same.

NOTES To make an Unbreakable Vow, two wizards must kneel opposite one another and clasp their right hands while another wizard acts as the Bonder.

Vera Verto

TYPE Transfiguration

PRONUNCIATION Vare-ah vare-toe

USE To transform animals into water goblets

ETYMOLOGY In Latin, *vera* means "true" and *verto* means "I turn."

MAGIC MOMENT In the *Chamber of Secrets* film, Minerva McGonagall taught this spell to her second-year students. During Ron's attempt at the spell, his goblet retained the tail of a rat.

NOTES This spell is performed by tapping the targeted animal three times with one's wand before pointing and reciting the incantation.

Verdillious

TYPE Conjuration

PRONUNCIATION *Ver-dill-ee-ous*

USE To conjure green sparks

ETYMOLOGY In Latin, *verde* means green.

PREFERRED MOVEMENT

MAGIC MOMENT In *Sorcerer's Stone*, Rubeus Hagrid told Harry, Hermione, Neville Longbottom and Draco Malfoy to send up Green Sparks if they found the unicorn in the Forbidden Forest.

NOTES This spell may be the same as Verdimillious.

Vermillious

TYPE Conjuration

PRONUNCIATION *Ver-mill-ee-ous*

USE To conjure red sparks

ETYMOLOGY In English, *vermilion* is a bright shade of red.

PREFERRED MOVEMENT

MAGIC MOMENT In the Third Task of the Triwizard Tournament, champions were advised to send up Red Sparks if they were lost or otherwise in need of dire help inside the maze.

NOTES In the *Harry Potter* video games, Vermillious Duo and Vermillious Tria are more powerful versions of this spell.

Vipera Evanesca

TYPE Untransfiguration

PRONUNCIATION *Vee-pair-uh eh-van-ess-ka*

USE To vanish a snake

ETYMOLOGY *Vipera* is a genus of venomous snakes. In Latin, *evanesco* means "disappear."

MAGIC MOMENT In *Chamber of Secrets*, Severus Snape uses this spell to vanish the snake that Draco Malfoy had conjured during a Dueling Club meeting.

NOTES In the *Deathly Hallows: Part 1* video game, Harry uses this spell to vanish a snake that crosses his path.

Vulnera Sanentur

TYPE Healing Spell

PRONUNCIATION *Vul-ner-ah sah-nen-tour*

USE To heal wounds created by Sectumsempra

ETYMOLOGY In Latin, *vulnus* means "wound" and *sanare* means "to heal."

MAGIC MOMENT In *Half-Blood Prince*, Severus Snape uses this spell to heal Draco Malfoy after Harry had injured him with Sectumsempra.

NOTES This spell was invented by Severus Snape. Though it is fully effective in healing wounds, dittany must be applied to prevent scarring.

✳ ✳ CHAPTER 2 ✳ ✳

CHARMS

All known charms in the Wizarding
World. Charms require precise wand
movements, correct pronunciation and
absolute concentration to be successful.

*charms alter what
an object is doing.*

Aberto

PRONUNCIATION *Uh-bear-toe*

USE To open locked doors

ETYMOLOGY In Portuguese, *aberto* means "open."

MAGIC MOMENT In the *Fantastic Beasts and Where to Find Them* film, Queenie Goldstein attempts to use this spell to get into Percival Graves's office. Unfortunately, he has locked it with more advanced magic.

NOTES According to the *Book of Spells* by Miranda Goshawk, the spell is a shortened version of Portaberto, a more aggressive door-opening spell commonly used before the invention of Alohomora.

Accio

PRONUNCIATION *Ak-see-oh* or *Ah-see-oh*

USE To summon objects

ETYMOLOGY In Latin, *accio* means "to call" or "to summon."

MAGIC MOMENT In *Goblet of Fire*, Harry Potter famously used this spell to summon his broom during the first task of the Triwizard Tournament.

PREFERRED WAND MOVEMENT

NOTES This spell can only be used on objects and small animals. At Hogwarts, this spell is first taught to fourth-years. The caster must concentrate on the object they are summoning in order for it to be successful. Anti-theft charms can be placed on objects in order to prevent them from being summoned; according to Goshawk's *Book of Spells*, most magical objects are sold pre-enchanted with such charms.

Age Line

PRONUNCIATION Incantation unknown

USE To prevent people under a certain age from crossing a set point

ETYMOLOGY N/A

MAGIC MOMENT In *Goblet of Fire*, Albus Dumbledore drew an Age Line to prevent underage students from entering the Triwizard Tournament.

> **NOTES** Age Lines cannot be tricked by Aging Potions.

See: the Weasley twins

Aguamenti

PRONUNCIATION Ah-gwah-men-tee

USE To produce clean, drinkable water

ETYMOLOGY In Spanish and Portuguese, *agua* means "water" and *mente* means "mind."

PREFERRED WAND MOVEMENT

MAGIC MOMENT In *Half-Blood Prince*, Harry uses this spell to refill the goblet which Dumbledore had drank potion out of while the two are in the Crystal Cave. However, it dried up before Dumbledore could drink it.

> **NOTES** Aguamenti cannot be used to extinguish Fiendfyre.

Alarte Ascendare

PRONUNCIATION *Ah-lar-tay ah-sen-der-ay*

USE To launch a target upward

ETYMOLOGY In Latin, *ala* means "wing" and *ascendare* means "to ascend."

MAGIC MOMENT In *Chamber of Secrets*, Gilderoy Lockhart uses this spell on the snake conjured by Draco Malfoy during the first meeting of Dueling Club. It is unclear what Lockhart's goal was, but this seemed to anger the snake.

NOTES In a moment of panic, Hermione uses this same spell five years later in *Deathly Hallows* against the serpent Nagini when the snake tried to kill Harry in Bathilda Bagshot's home.

Alohomora

PRONUNCIATION *Ah-low-ho-more-ah*

USE To unlock doors and windows

ETYMOLOGY According to J.K. Rowling, the word is from a West African word that means "friendly to thieves."

PREFERRED WAND MOVEMENT

MAGIC MOMENT In *Cursed Child*, Scorpius Malfoy uses this to break into the Minister for Magic's office. Surprisingly, it works.

NOTES Also known as the Thief's Friend, the invention of this charm offered a much subtler way to open doors than the likes of Aberto or Open Sesame.

Anti-Cheating Spell

PRONUNCIATION Unknown

USE To prevent cheating

ETYMOLOGY N/A

MAGIC MOMENT In *Sorcerer's Stone*, Hermione informs Ron he cannot cheat off her during the final examinations because their quills will be bewitched with an Anti-Cheating Spell.

NOTES An Anti-Cheating Spell can be rendered useless by casting a Cribbing Spell.

Aparecium

PRONUNCIATION Ah-par-ee-cee-um

USE To reveal invisible ink or other hidden messages

ETYMOLOGY In Latin, *appareo* means "to become visible or appear."

PREFERRED WAND MOVEMENT

MAGIC MOMENT In *Chamber of Secrets*, Hermione attempted to use this spell on Tom Riddle's diary.

NOTES May be related to Revelio.

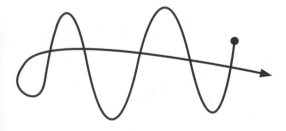

Aqua Eructo

PRONUNCIATION *Ah-kwa ee-ruck-toe*

USE To conjure water

ETYMOLOGY In Latin, *aqua* means "water" and *eructo* means "erupt."

MAGIC MOMENT In the *Goblet of Fire* video game, Barty Crouch Jr.—disguised as Alastor Moody—teaches fourth-year students at Hogwarts how to perform this charm.

NOTES May be related to the Extinguishing Charm, as it is mostly used to put out fires.

Arresto Momentum

PRONUNCIATION *Ah-rest-toe moe-men-tum*

USE To slow or stop a moving target

ETYMOLOGY In Old French, *arester* means "stop," and in Latin, *momentum* means "movement."

MAGIC MOMENT According to *Pottermore*, this spell was used during the 2014 Quidditch World Cup to keep a falling Jamaican player from hitting the ground.

NOTES Albus Dumbledore also uses this spell to keep Harry from getting hurt on the Quidditch pitch in the *Prisoner of Azkaban* film.

Ascendio

PRONUNCIATION *Ah-sen-dee-oh*

USE To propel the caster upwards

ETYMOLOGY In Latin, *ascendere* means "to climb."

MAGIC MOMENT In the *Goblet of Fire* film, Harry uses this charm to reach the surface of the Hogwarts lake during the second task.

> **NOTES** Newt Scamander also uses this charm in *Fantastic Beasts: The Crimes of Grindelwald* while attempting to escape a pack of Matagots.

Baubillious

PRONUNCIATION *Baw-bill-ee-us*

USE To shoot lightning

ETYMOLOGY Likely from the English *bauble*, meaning "a shiny ornament."

MAGIC MOMENT In the *Harry Potter Trading Card Game*, Filius Flitwick performs this spell.

> **NOTES** Though the name of this charm seems to reference Flitwick decorating the Great Hall's Christmas tree in *Sorcerer's Stone*, its trading card instructs the user to "do one damage to your opponent or to a creature of your choice," implying it is used for dueling.

Bewitched Snowballs

PRONUNCIATION Unknown

USE To charm snowballs to continually hit a target

ETYMOLOGY N/A

MAGIC MOMENT In *Sorcerer's Stone*, Fred and George Weasley are punished for using this charm to pelt snowballs at the back of Quirinus Quirrell's turban.

aka Lord Voldemort

NOTES Fred and George may have used this same spell in *Order of the Phoenix* when they annoyed Ron by charming snowballs to repeatedly hit the Gryffindor Common Room window.

Bombarda

PRONUNCIATION *Bom-bar-da*

USE To create an explosion

ETYMOLOGY In English, *bombard* means "attack."

MAGIC MOMENT In *Cursed Child*, Albus Potter considers this charm as a means to destroy the Time-Turner.

NOTES In the *Order of the Phoenix* film, a more powerful version of the spell, Bombarda Maxima, is used by Dolores Umbridge to break into the Room of Requirement.

Bubble-Head Charm

PRONUNCIATION Unknown

USE To create a protective bubble around one's head, allowing for continual supply of oxygen

ETYMOLOGY N/A

MAGIC MOMENT Both Cedric Diggory and Fleur Delacour chose to use this charm for the second task of the Triwizard Tournament, which required the champions to stay underwater for up to one hour.

NOTES This spell is also useful for avoiding noxious smells, as evidenced by its popularity among Hogwarts students when Dungbombs and Stink Pellets became a common form of rebellion against Dolores Umbridge.

Carpe Retractum

PRONUNCIATION Kahr-pay ruh-track-tum

USE To pull a target toward the caster, or the caster toward a target

ETYMOLOGY In Latin, carpe means "seize" and retractum means "remote."

MAGIC MOMENT Filius Flitwick teaches this spell to third-year students in the Prisoner of Azkaban video game.

NOTES This spell is only mentioned in the Prisoner of Azkaban and Goblet of Fire video games.

Caterwauling Charm

PRONUNCIATION Unknown

USE To set off a high-pitched shriek if unauthorized persons enter the area

ETYMOLOGY N/A

MAGIC MOMENT In *Deathly Hallows*, Harry, Ron and Hermione inadvertently set off the Caterwauling Charm that Death Eaters had placed in order to enforce a curfew in Hogsmeade.

NOTES There is no way of proving who set off a Caterwauling Charm, as Aberforth Dumbledore was able to convince the Death Eaters he had done so when he put out his cat.

Or maybe Death Eaters aren't very bright...

Cave Inimicum

PRONUNCIATION Kah-vay uh-nim-i-kuhm

USE To keep enemies away

ETYMOLOGY In Latin, *Cave Inimicum* is a phrase meaning "beware of the enemy."

MAGIC MOMENT Hermione regularly used this spell to protect herself, Ron and Harry while on the hunt for Horcruxes in *Deathly Hallows*.

NOTES Those behind this spell's shield will not be seen, heard or even smelled if the spell is well-cast. It is unclear whether this spell is used or has a less effective shield in the *Deathly Hallows* films, as a Death Eater is able to smell Hermione's perfume through her protective spells.

Cheering Charm

PRONUNCIATION Unknown

USE To make the target happy

ETYMOLOGY N/A

MAGIC MOMENT In *Prisoner of Azkaban*, third-years were tested on this spell for their end-of-year exams. Harry's Cheering Charm was a bit too strong, causing Ron, his partner, to be led to a quiet room until his fits of hysterical laughter had subsided.

NOTES According to a "Wizard of the Month" feature on J.K. Rowling's official website, Felix Summerbee invented this spell in the 1400s.

Colloportus

PRONUNCIATION *Cull-low-pore-tuss*

USE To lock doors so they cannot be opened manually

ETYMOLOGY In Latin, *colligo* means "to bind together" and *portus* means "door."

PREFERRED MOVEMENT

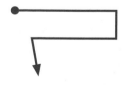

MAGIC MOMENT Luna Lovegood, Neville Longbottom, Hermione and Harry all used this spell during the Battle of the Department of Mysteries.

NOTES This spell can be easily countered by Alohomora.

Color Change Charm

PRONUNCIATION Unknown

USE To change color of a target

ETYMOLOGY N/A

MAGIC MOMENT In *Order of the Phoenix*, Harry mixes this up with the Growth Charm during his Charms O.W.L.—the rat he was supposed to be turning orange had become the size of a badger before he could correct his mistake.

NOTES This spell may be a variation of Colovaria, a color-changing spell mentioned in the *LEGO Harry Potter* video games.

Confundo

PRONUNCIATION *Con-fun-doh*

USE To produce confusion in the target

ETYMOLOGY In Latin, *confundere* means "to confuse."

PREFERRED MOVEMENT

MAGIC MOMENT In *Cursed Child*, Ron admits to Harry that he passed his Muggle driving test by Confunding the instructor.

NOTES Inanimate objects that have "minds" can also be Confunded, such as when Barty Crouch Jr. performed this spell on the Goblet of Fire.

Defodio

PRONUNCIATION Deh-foh-dee-oh

USE To gouge out portions of earth or stone

ETYMOLOGY In Latin, *defodio* means "dig out."

PREFERRED MOVEMENT

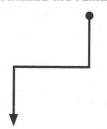

MAGIC MOMENT In *Deathly Hallows*, Harry, Ron and Hermione use this spell while escaping Gringotts on the back of a blind dragon.

> **NOTES** Also known as the Gouging Spell. According to Miranda Goshawk's *Book of Spells*, "From budding Herbologists digging for Snargaluff seedlings to treasure-hunting curse breakers uncovering ancient wizard tombs, the Gouging Spell makes all manner of heavy labour a matter of pointing a wand."

Deletrius

PRONUNCIATION De-lee-tree-us

USE To cause the target to disintegrate

ETYMOLOGY In Latin, *delere* means "to destroy."

MAGIC MOMENT In *Goblet of Fire*, Amos Diggory uses this spell to get rid of the ghost image of the Dark Mark caused by performing a Reverse Spell on Harry's wand.

> **NOTES** This spell is also known as the Eradication Spell.

Deprimo

PRONUNCIATION *Dee-primo-oh*

USE To blast holes downward

ETYMOLOGY In Latin, *deprimo* means "dig deep."

MAGIC MOMENT In *Deathly Hallows*, Hermione uses this spell to blast a hole through the floor of Xenophilius Lovegood's house, allowing her, Ron and Harry to escape after Lovegood had tried to turn them over to Death Eaters.

NOTES This spell is also used in the *Sorcerer's Stone* video game.

Depulso

PRONUNCIATION *De-puhl-so*

USE To move a target away

ETYMOLOGY In Latin, *depulsio* means "push away."

MAGIC MOMENT Harry, Ron, Hermione and the rest of the fourth-years practice this spell during their Charms class in *Goblet of Fire*.

NOTES Also known as a Banishing Charm. This charm works on whatever object it is pointed at, even if it was not the object the caster intended to banish.

As when Neville Longbottom banished Flitwick across the Charms classroom

Descendo

PRONUNCIATION Deh-sen-do

USE To lower a target

ETYMOLOGY In Latin, *descendo* means "I descend."

MAGIC MOMENT In *Deathly Hallows*, Ron uses this spell to lower the ceiling hatch and ladder to access the Burrow's attic. Inside was the family's ghoul, which they had transfigured to look like Ron with a case of spattergroit.

> **NOTES** Descendo can be countered with the General Counter-Spell, Finite.

Diffindo

PRONUNCIATION Dee-fin-doh

USE To sever a target

ETYMOLOGY In Latin, *diffindo* means "I split" or "I cleave."

PREFERRED MOVEMENT

MAGIC MOMENT In *Goblet of Fire*, Ron uses this spell to remove the lace sleeves from his dress robes before attending the Yule Ball.

> **NOTES** According to Miranda Goshawk's *Book of Spells*, Diffindo was invented in the 15th century by a seamstress named Delfina Crimp.

Diminuendo

PRONUNCIATION *Dih-min-you-en-doh*

USE To make objects shrink

ETYMOLOGY In Italian, *diminuendo* means "diminishing."

MAGIC MOMENT In the *Order of the Phoenix* film, Nigel Wolpert uses this spell during a Dumbledore's Army meeting in the Room of Requirement.

NOTES This spell may be related to the Shrinking Charm, Reducio.

Disillusionment Charm

Feels like someone broke an egg on your head.

PRONUNCIATION Unknown

USE To disguise a target to perfectly match surroundings

ETYMOLOGY N/A

MAGIC MOMENT In *Order of the Phoenix*, Alastor Moody casts this spell on Harry to protect him while they traveled from the Dursley home to 12 Grimmauld Place.

NOTES According to the book *Fantastic Beasts and Where to Find Them*, Hippogriffs and winged horses may be kept by wizards as long as they cast daily Disillusionment Charms on them.

Dissendium

PRONUNCIATION *Diss-en-dee-um*

USE To reveal secret passageways

ETYMOLOGY Likely from Latin *dissocio*, meaning "to part" or "to separate."

MAGIC MOMENT In *Prisoner of Azkaban*, Harry uses this spell to reveal a secret passageway out of Hogwarts behind the statue of a one-eyed witch with a humpback.

NOTES This spell was revealed to Harry by the Marauder's Map.

Drought Charm

PRONUNCIATION Unknown

USE To dry up puddles and ponds

ETYMOLOGY N/A

MAGIC MOMENT In *Goblet of Fire*, Ron found this charm while looking up ways for Harry to survive the second task of the Triwizard Tournament.

NOTES According to Ron's research, this charm would not have been nearly strong enough to remove all the water from the Great Lake.

Duro

PRONUNCIATION *Duhr-oh*

USE To turn the target into stone

ETYMOLOGY In Latin, *duro* means "to harden."

PREFERRED WAND MOVEMENT

MAGIC MOMENT In *Deathly Hallows*, Hermione uses this charm on a tapestry that two Death Eaters were about to run into during the Battle of Hogwarts.

> **NOTES** This was first identified as a Hardening Charm in the *Wonderbook: Book of Spells* video game.

Emancipare

PRONUNCIATION *Ee-man-cee-par-ay*

USE To release bindings

ETYMOLOGY From Latin *emancipare*, meaning "to free from control."

MAGIC MOMENT In *Cursed Child*, after Harry duels with Draco Malfoy and uses the binding spell Brachiabindo, Draco frees himself with this counter-charm.

> **NOTES** This can also be used as a counter-charm against Fulgari.

Engorgio

PRONUNCIATION *En-gorg-ee-oh*

USE To cause target to swell

ETYMOLOGY In English, the word *engorge* means "to swell with fluid" or "eat to excess."

PREFERRED WAND MOVEMENT

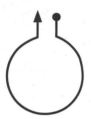

MAGIC MOMENT In *Chamber of Secrets*, Hermione suspects that Hagrid illegally used an Engorgement Charm to enhance the size of his pumpkins.

> **NOTES** This spell is also known as an Engorgement Charm or Growing Charm.

this spell is not recommended for slugs.

Erecto

PRONUNCIATION *Eh-rek-toe*

USE To erect a structure

ETYMOLOGY In Latin, *erectum* means "to have erected."

MAGIC MOMENT In *Deathly Hallows*, Harry, Ron and Hermione regularly use this spell to put up their camping tent.

> **NOTES** This spell is only seen being used on tents, but it could presumably put up any structure.

Expecto Patronum

PRONUNCIATION *Ex-pec-toe pah-tro-num*

USE To conjure a Patronus

ETYMOLOGY In Latin, *expecto* means "I wait for" and *patronus* means "protector" or "guardian."

MAGIC MOMENT In *Prisoner of Azkaban*, Harry learns this extremely difficult charm from Remus Lupin in order to defend himself against Dementors.

NOTES Patronuses are known for being used to defend against creatures such as Dementors and Lethifolds, but they can also be used to send messages, as shown by Order of the Phoenix members Arthur Weasley and Kingsley Shacklebolt. A Patronus can be very personal—Harry's takes the shape of his father's Animagus form, a stag.

Expelliarmus

PRONUNCIATION *Ex-pell-ee-arm-us*

USE To disarm the target

ETYMOLOGY In Latin, *expellere* means "to drive out" and *arma* means "weapon."

PREFERRED WAND MOVEMENT

MAGIC MOMENT During the Battle of the Seven Potters in *Deathly Hallows*, Harry uses this spell to disarm Stan Shunpike, who was working for Voldemort under the Imperius Curse. This revealed the "real" Harry to the Death Eaters, who knew this spell to be his calling card.

NOTES This spell is mostly used to disarm an opponent's wand but will cause anything the target is holding to fly out of their hands.

Feather-Light Charm

PRONUNCIATION Unknown

USE To make heavy objects feather-light

ETYMOLOGY N/A

MAGIC MOMENT In *Prisoner of Azkaban*, Harry believes he is a fugitive after having blown up his Aunt Marge and considers bewitching his trunk with such a charm so he can tie it to his broomstick and go to Gringotts.

NOTES It is unclear why Hogwarts students would not regularly use this charm on their belongings. Presumably, it would be illegal under the Decree for the Reasonable Restriction of Underage Sorcery.

Fianto Duri

PRONUNCIATION Fee-ahn-toe dyur-ee

USE Allows a caster to keep one charm active while casting other spells

ETYMOLOGY In Latin, *fiant* means "done" and *duri* means "lasts."

MAGIC MOMENT In the *Deathly Hallows* film, Filius Flitwick uses this spell to reinforce Protego Maxima (a Shield Charm that would normally require the caster's continuous focus), which he had cast to protect Hogwarts Castle.

NOTES In the film version, Flitwick is joined by Molly Weasley and Horace Slughorn in casting these protective enchantments.

Fidelius Charm

PRONUNCIATION Unknown

USE To conceal information inside a single living soul, who is then known as a Secret Keeper

ETYMOLOGY In Latin, *fidelis* means "trustworthy."

MAGIC MOMENT This charm was used to protect the location of the Potter home from Lord Voldemort, with Peter Pettigrew acting as Secret Keeper. Pettigrew betrayed the Potters, leading to the deaths of James and Lily.

Never trust a rat.

NOTES Anyone who the primary Keeper divulges the secret to becomes a secondary Keeper. Secondary Keepers cannot tell the protected secret to anyone else, even if they want to. In the event of a Secret Keeper's death, any secondary Keepers become primary Keepers.

Finestra

PRONUNCIATION Fin-es-tra

USE To shatter a window into dust

ETYMOLOGY In Italian, *finestra* means "window."

MAGIC MOMENT In the *Fantastic Beasts and Where to Find Them* film, Newt Scamander uses this spell on a store window while trying to recapture his escaped Niffler.

NOTES This is a considerate choice for destroying a window, as it doesn't leave behind broken glass.

Flame-Freezing Charm

PRONUNCIATION Unknown

USE To make fire feel like a warm summer breeze

ETYMOLOGY N/A

MAGIC MOMENT In *Prisoner of Azkaban*, Harry reads about how medieval witches and wizards would use this spell and feign pain if they were ever being burned at the stake.

NOTES One witch known as Wendelin the Weird enjoyed the effects of this spell so much that she wore various disguises and allowed herself to be caught and burned at least 47 times.

Fulgari

PRONUNCIATION *Ful-gar-ee*

USE To bind an opponent's arms in luminous cords

ETYMOLOGY In Latin, *fulgur* means "lightning."

MAGIC MOMENT In *Cursed Child*, Delphini uses this on Albus Potter and Scorpius Malfoy before forcing them to time travel to the third task of the Triwizard Tournament in 1995.

NOTES This charm can be countered with Emancipare.

Glacius

PRONUNCIATION *Glay-see-us*

USE To freeze the air in front of the wand

ETYMOLOGY In Latin, *glacius* means "ice."

MAGIC MOMENT In the *LEGO Harry Potter* video games, Remus Lupin teaches this spell to third-year students.

NOTES Glacius Duo and Glacius Tria are more powerful versions of this spell.

Glisseo

PRONUNCIATION *Gliss-ee-oh*

USE To flatten a staircase into a slide

ETYMOLOGY In French, *glisser* means "to slide."

MAGIC MOMENT In *Deathly Hallows*, Hermione uses this spell to enable herself, Ron and Harry to quickly evade Death Eaters during the Battle of Hogwarts.

NOTES This may be the same spell used to enchant the staircase to the girls' dormitory in Gryffindor Tower.

Gripping Charm

PRONUNCIATION Unknown

USE To make objects easier to grip

ETYMOLOGY N/A

MAGIC MOMENT According to *Quidditch Through the Ages*, this charm made straps and finger holes on Quaffles unnecessary.

NOTES This charm was discovered in 1875.

Hair-Thickening Charm

PRONUNCIATION Unknown

USE To make hair grow quickly

ETYMOLOGY N/A

MAGIC MOMENT In *Order of the Phoenix*, a Slytherin student cast this spell on Alicia Spinnet, causing her eyebrows to grow at an alarming rate. This was one of a few incidents in which Slytherin students targeted members of the Gryffindor Quidditch team.

NOTES This may be the spell Harry unknowingly used as a child after Petunia Dursley gave him a terrible haircut.

Harmonia Nectere Passus

PRONUNCIATION
Har-moh-nia neck-tar-ay pass-us

USE To repair Vanishing Cabinets

ETYMOLOGY In Latin, *harmonia* means
"harmony," *nectere* means "connect
together" and *passus* can mean "spread out,"
"extended" or "open."

MAGIC MOMENT In the *Half-Blood Prince*
film, Draco Malfoy uses this spell while
repairing the Vanishing Cabinet in the Room
of Requirement.

NOTES It's possible that these
were three separate spells Draco used in
his efforts to repair the cabinet, as it took
him almost the entire school year to fix.

Herbivicus

PRONUNCIATION Her-biv-ih-cuss

USE To increase plant growth and cause
flowers to bloom

ETYMOLOGY Likely a Latinization of the
English *herb*.

MAGIC MOMENT In the *Goblet of Fire*
video game, this spell could be found in a
spellbook owned by Pomona Sprout.

NOTES Herbivicus Duo is a more powerful version of this charm.

Homonculous Charm

PRONUNCIATION Unknown

USE To allow an object to track the movements of people

ETYMOLOGY *Homunculus* is a term used to refer to the representation of a human.

MAGIC MOMENT The Marauder's Map is enchanted with a Homonculous Charm, enabling it to keep track of every person on Hogwarts grounds.

NOTES The spell cannot be fooled by Polyjuice Potions, Invisibility Cloaks or Animagi. It can also label cats, such as Mrs. Norris.

Homorphus Charm

PRONUNCIATION *Ho-morf-us*

USE To temporarily return a werewolf to his human form

ETYMOLOGY From the Latin *homo*, meaning "man," and the Greek *morphe*, meaning "shape."

MAGIC MOMENT Gilderoy Lockhart claimed to have used this spell to defeat the Wagga Wagga Werewolf. In fact, the credit belongs to an Armenian warlock.

What a surprise.

NOTES Lockhart claimed this spell permanently cures lycanthropy, but this is incorrect.

Horton-Keitch Braking Charm

PRONUNCIATION Unknown

USE To let broomsticks stop more precisely

ETYMOLOGY N/A

MAGIC MOMENT *Quidditch Through the Ages* explains that this charm made players less likely to overshoot goals or fly offside.

NOTES This spell was invented by Basil Horton and Randolph Keitch, c. 1929. It's standard on all broomsticks made by the Comet Trading Company.

Hour-Reversal Charm

PRONUNCIATION Unknown

USE To reverse time

ETYMOLOGY N/A

MAGIC MOMENT In *Prisoner of Azkaban*, Hermione and Harry use this spell via a Time-Turner to save both Buckbeak and Sirius Black.

NOTES Time-Turners were invented to use this spell, which benefits from containment. On its own, the spell is unstable.

Hover Charm

PRONUNCIATION Unknown

USE To cause objects to hover

ETYMOLOGY N/A

PREFERRED MOVEMENT

MAGIC MOMENT In *Chamber of Secrets*, Dobby uses this charm to make Petunia Dursley's pudding float and then crash to the floor.

NOTES This spell makes objects hover statically, unlike Wingardium Leviosa, which makes objects fly up.

Illegibilus

PRONUNCIATION Ill-eg-ih-bill-us

USE To make a text unreadable

ETYMOLOGY In English, *illegible* means "unreadable."

MAGIC MOMENT This spell is only mentioned in the *Harry Potter Trading Card Game*.

NOTES This may be useful for concealing a document's information from others.

Immobulus

PRONUNCIATION Ih-moh-byoo-lus

USE To render a target immobile

ETYMOLOGY In Latin, *immobilis* means "unmoving."

PREFERRED WAND MOVEMENT

MAGIC MOMENT In the *Prisoner of Azkaban* film, Remus Lupin uses this Freezing Charm to immobilize the Whomping Willow.

> **NOTES** According to Horace Slughorn, a Freezing Charm can disable a Muggle burglar alarm.

Imperturbable Charm

PRONUNCIATION Unknown

USE To create a magical barrier around the target

ETYMOLOGY N/A

MAGIC MOMENT In *Order of the Phoenix*, Molly Weasley places this charm on a door so that Harry, Hermione and the Weasley children cannot listen to the Order's conversations.

> **NOTES** This charm blocks both noise and objects—the twins' Extendable Ears could not go under a door that had been Imperturbed.

Impervius

PRONUNCIATION *Im-pur-vee-us*

USE To make the target repel water and mist

ETYMOLOGY In English, *impervious* means "not penetrable."

MAGIC MOMENT In *Prisoner of Azkaban*, Hermione uses this spell on Harry's glasses so he can see during a rainy Quidditch match.

NOTES In *Deathly Hallows*, Hermione also suggested Ron use this charm to protect the things in Corban Yaxley's office until he could sort out the rain.

Inflatus

PRONUNCIATION *In-flay-tuss*

USE To inflate a target

ETYMOLOGY In English, *inflate* means "expand with air."

MAGIC MOMENT In the *Goblet of Fire* video game, Harry, Ron and Hermione use this spell on creatures found on Hogwarts grounds.

NOTES This spell can be used to increase the size of a target. If the target reaches capacity, it will explode into balloons.

Informous

PRONUNCIATION *In-form-us*

USE To add information on a creature to the caster's *Folio Bruti*, or *Book of Beasts*

ETYMOLOGY In English, *inform* means "to communicate knowledge."

MAGIC MOMENT This spell is used in the *Chamber of Secrets* and *Prisoner of Azkaban* video games.

NOTES Information about a magical creature's strengths and weaknesses can be useful in future encounters.

Intruder Charm

PRONUNCIATION Unknown

USE To detect intruders and set off an alarm

ETYMOLOGY N/A

MAGIC MOMENT In *Half-Blood Prince*, Horace Slughorn uses this charm on a Muggle house he is staying in.

NOTES The alarm is presumably not very loud, as Slughorn is in the bath when Harry and Albus Dumbledore arrive and does not hear it go off.

Invisibility Spell

PRONUNCIATION Unknown

USE To make an object invisible

ETYMOLOGY N/A

MAGIC MOMENT In *Order of the Phoenix*, Hermione comments that Fred and George Weasley's Headless Hats were very clever for having extended an Invisibility Spell's effects beyond the enchanted object.

NOTES Revelio may be a counter-spell for this charm.

Locomotor

PRONUNCIATION *Loh-koh-moh-tor*

USE To move a target

ETYMOLOGY In Latin, *loco* means "place" and *moto* means "moving."

MAGIC MOMENT In the *Fantastic Beasts and Where to Find Them* film, Porpentina Goldstein uses this charm to set a table for dinner.

NOTES It is common to follow Locomotor with a target word, such as "Locomotor trunk."

Lumos

PRONUNCIATION *Loo-mos*

USE To light the tip of the wand

ETYMOLOGY In Latin, *lumen* means "light."

PREFERRED MOVEMENT

MAGIC MOMENT In *Goblet of Fire*, Albus Dumbledore uses this spell while searching for Barty Crouch Sr. around the edges of the Forbidden Forest.

> **NOTES** In the *Prisoner of Azkaban* film, Lumos Maxima is a more powerful version of this charm.

Lumos Solem

PRONUNCIATION *Loo-mos so-lem*

USE To create a narrow beam of light

ETYMOLOGY In Latin, *lumen* means "light" and *solis* means "of the sun."

MAGIC MOMENT In the *Sorcerer's Stone* film, Hermione uses this spell to free Ron from the Devil's Snare.

> **NOTES** In the book, Hermione used the Bluebell Flames spell to free Ron and Harry from the deadly plant.

Metelojinx

PRONUNCIATION *Meh-tel-oh-jinx*

USE To create a localized thunderstorm

ETYMOLOGY In Greek, *meteoros* refers to anything that falls from the sky.

MAGIC MOMENT This spell is occasionally used at the Wizarding World of Harry Potter.

NOTES This charm is very similar to Meteolojinx, which is sometimes used at the Wizarding World of Harry Potter Japan to create a snow storm.

Mobiliarbus

PRONUNCIATION *Mo-bi-lee-ar-bus*

USE To move trees and other wooden targets

ETYMOLOGY In Latin, *mobilis* means "movable" and *arbor* means "tree."

MAGIC MOMENT In *Prisoner of Azkaban*, Hermione uses this charm to shift a Christmas tree, blocking herself, Ron and Harry from the view of others in the Three Broomsticks.

NOTES "Mobili" can likely move a range of objects if the caster knows the correct Latin suffix.

Mobilicorpus

PRONUNCIATION *Mo-bi-lee-kor-pus*

USE To move bodies

ETYMOLOGY In Latin, *mobilis* means "movable" and *corpus* means "body."

MAGIC MOMENT In *Prisoner of Azkaban*, Remus Lupin uses this spell to move an unconscious Snape out of the Shrieking Shack.

NOTES When in use, this spell hoists up a body with "invisible strings," as if it were a puppet.

Molliare

PRONUNCIATION *Moll-ee-are-ay*

USE To create a softening effect on the target

ETYMOLOGY In Latin, *mollire* means "to soften."

MAGIC MOMENT According to *Quidditch Through the Ages*, this charm is largely used in broomstick production to make them more comfortable.

NOTES Also known as the Cushioning Charm, it was invented by Elliot Smethwyck in 1820.

Muffliato

PRONUNCIATION Muff-lee-ah-toe

USE To fill the ears of those nearby with a buzzing noise

ETYMOLOGY In English, to *muffle* means "to deaden sound."

MAGIC MOMENT Harry used this charm often after learning it from the Half-Blood Prince's copy of *Advanced Potion-Making*.

NOTES Hermione initially disapproved of this spell's usage and refused to speak if Harry cast it during their sixth year.

Nox

PRONUNCIATION Nocks

USE To extinguish a wand lit by Lumos

ETYMOLOGY In Latin, *nox* means "night."

PREFERRED MOVEMENT

MAGIC MOMENT In *Deathly Hallows*, Harry uses this spell to extinguish his wand as he approached the Shrieking Shack, where Voldemort was overseeing the Battle of Hogwarts.

NOTES This is also known as the Wand-Extinguishing Charm.

Obliteration Charm

PRONUNCIATION Unknown

USE To remove tracks

ETYMOLOGY N/A

MAGIC MOMENT In *Order of the Phoenix*, Hermione uses this charm to remove the footprints she, Ron and Harry made in the snow on their way back from Hagrid's cabin.

> **NOTES** Hermione may have used this same spell to hide the footprints they left while in Godric's Hollow.

Obliviate

PRONUNCIATION *Oh-bli-vee-ate*

USE To erase a target's memories

ETYMOLOGY In Latin, *oblivisci* means "forget."

PREFERRED MOVEMENT

MAGIC MOMENT In *Chamber of Secrets*, Gilderoy Lockhart attempts to use this spell on Ron and Harry. It backfires due to his use of Ron's damaged wand, and Lockhart ends up in St. Mungo's Hospital with permanent memory damage.

> **NOTES** The Ministry of Magic regularly uses this spell to modify the memories of Muggles who have seen evidence of the Wizarding World.

Oculus Reparo

PRONUNCIATION *Ock-you-lus reh-pah-roh*

USE To repair eyeglasses

ETYMOLOGY In Latin, *oculus* means "eye" and *reparo* means "repair."

MAGIC MOMENT In the *Sorcerer's Stone* film, Hermione uses this charm to fix Harry's glasses on the Hogwarts Express.

> **NOTES** This is a variation of the Reparo charm.

Pack

PRONUNCIATION *Pack*

USE To pack luggage

ETYMOLOGY N/A

MAGIC MOMENT In *Order of the Phoenix*, Nymphadora Tonks uses this spell to quickly pack Harry's belongings in his trunk before they left for 12 Grimmauld Place.

> **NOTES** Casters who are more skilled at housework spells may be able to execute this spell more neatly; Tonks mentioned that her mother was capable of making socks fold themselves up.

"Pack" is an unusual incantation-Tonks might have used a different nonverbal spell.

Partis Temporus

PRONUNCIATION *Par-tus tem-por-us*

USE To temporarily divide a target

ETYMOLOGY In Latin, *partio* means "divide" and *temporarius* means "temporary."

MAGIC MOMENT In the *Half-Blood Prince* film, Albus Dumbledore uses this spell to part the Firestorm flames he had just cast to drive off the Inferi.

NOTES In the book version, Dumbledore does not use this spell but has the flames serve as a shield as he and Harry make their way back to the boat.

Permanent Sticking Charm

PRONUNCIATION Unknown

USE To permanently attach one object to another

ETYMOLOGY N/A

MAGIC MOMENT Sirius Black believes his mother used a Permanent Sticking Charm to mount a painting of herself to a wall in 12 Grimmauld Place.

NOTES Unlike many other spells, a Permanent Sticking Charm's effects seem to last even after its caster dies.

Peskipiksi Pesternomi

PRONUNCIATION *Pesky-pixie pester-no-me*

USE To capture or repel pixies (allegedly)

ETYMOLOGY Likely derived from English *pesky pixie pester no me.*

you've got to be kidding me.

MAGIC MOMENT In *Chamber of Secrets,* Gilderoy Lockhart attempts to use this spell against pixies he had set loose in his own classroom.

> **NOTES** In the *Order of the Phoenix* film, the Theory of Charms O.W.L. asked whether this was a real charm and, if not, to conjure up the correct Latin terminology.

Piertotum Locomotor

PRONUNCIATION
Pee-air-toe-tum loh-koh-moh-tor

USE To animate statues and armor

ETYMOLOGY From the French *pierre,* meaning "stone," and the Latin *totum,* meaning "total."

MAGIC MOMENT In *Deathly Hallows,* Minerva McGonagall uses this spell to animate the statues and suits of armor throughout Hogwarts.

> **NOTES** This charm is a variation of Locomotor, though the targets become animated instead of simply moving where the caster directs them. This may be unique to the Hogwarts suits of armor and statues, as McGonagall instructs them to "do your duty to our school!"

Placement Charm

PRONUNCIATION Unknown

USE To place an object in a specific location

ETYMOLOGY N/A

MAGIC MOMENT In *Fantastic Beasts and Where to Find Them*, it is advised to use this charm to place a bridle on a kelpie. This is the only way to control a kelpie.

NOTES This charm is only mentioned in *Fantastic Beasts and Where to Find Them*.

Portus

PRONUNCIATION *Pour-tuss*

USE To turn an object into a Portkey

ETYMOLOGY In Latin, *porta* means "gate."

MAGIC MOMENT In *Order of the Phoenix*, Albus Dumbledore turns a kettle into a Portkey to 12 Grimmauld Place after Harry has a vision of Arthur Weasley being attacked by a snake.

NOTES The targeted object will briefly glow blue and tremble before appearing normal again.

Prior Incantato

PRONUNCIATION *Pry-or in-can-tah-to*

USE To force a wand to show an "echo" of the previous spell it has performed

ETYMOLOGY In Latin, *prior* means "earlier" and *incantatare* means "to enchant."

MAGIC MOMENT In *Goblet of Fire*, Amos Diggory uses this spell on Harry's wand to prove it was used to cast a Dark Mark in the sky.

> **NOTES** In rare instances when two wands with cores from the same animal are forced to duel against one another, this will manifest in Priori Incantatem. When one wand overpowers the other, it will force the losing wand to regurgitate "echoes" of the most recent spells it has cast.

If a killing curse is "echoed," a ghostlike form of the person killed will emerge from the wand.

Protean Charm

PRONUNCIATION Unknown

USE To link objects

ETYMOLOGY From the Greek *Proteus*, who was a shapeshifting god.

MAGIC MOMENT Inspired by the Death Eaters' Dark Marks, Hermione used this charm on fake Galleons as a way to alert members of Dumbledore's Army of the next meeting time.

> **NOTES** When the master coin was transfigured, the rest of the coins grew warm to alert the other D.A. members. This is similar to how the Death Eaters' Dark Marks will all burn when one touches their own Mark.

Protego

PRONUNCIATION *Pro-tay-go*

USE To make a magical shield that blocks both physical objects and spells

ETYMOLOGY In Latin, *protego* means "I protect."

PREFERRED MOVEMENT

MAGIC MOMENT In *Goblet of Fire*, Hermione and Ron help Harry practice this charm in preparation for the third task of the Triwizard Tournament. At one point, Hermione shatters Harry's shield with a "well-placed Jelly-Legs Jinx."

NOTES Protego is the simplest form of a Shield Charm and is good for protecting against minor to moderate jinxes, hexes and curses. Protego Horribilis, Protego Maxima and Protego Totalum are all more powerful versions of this charm.

Quietus

PRONUNCIATION *Kwy-uh-tus*

USE To reverse the effect of Sonorus

ETYMOLOGY In Latin, *quietus* means "quiet."

MAGIC MOMENT In *Goblet of Fire*, Ludo Bagman uses this charm to return his speaking voice to a normal volume after addressing the crowds at the Quidditch World Cup.

NOTES No light is emitted from one's wand when casting this spell.

Reducio

PRONUNCIATION *Ruh-doo-see-oh*

USE To make a target smaller

ETYMOLOGY In Latin, *reducio* means "reduce."

PREFERRED MOVEMENT

MAGIC MOMENT In *Goblet of Fire*, Barty Crouch Jr. uses this spell on an Engorged spider to return it to its normal size.

> **NOTES** In Miranda Goshawk's *Book of Spells*, this charm is taught along with Engorgio so students can return Engorged objects to their normal size.

Refilling Charm

PRONUNCIATION Unknown

USE To refill a vessel with whatever drink was originally in the container

ETYMOLOGY N/A

MAGIC MOMENT In *Half-Blood Prince*, Harry successfully casts this charm nonverbally to refill the wine glasses of Rubeus Hagrid and Horace Slughorn, even though he had never pulled it off before.

> **NOTES** This charm will not work with food, which is a Principal Exception of Gamp's Law of Elemental Transfiguration and therefore cannot be conjured.

(It helps when you've just taken a swig of Felix Felicis.)

Rennervate

PRONUNCIATION *Ren-nur-vayte*

USE To revive a target, especially one who has been stunned

ETYMOLOGY In Latin, *re* means "again" and *nervus* means "nerve."

MAGIC MOMENT In *Goblet of Fire*, Amos Diggory uses this spell to revive Winky after the Quidditch World Cup.

NOTES This spell was originally called "Enervate." When it was pointed out *enervate* is an English word that means "to weaken," J.K. Rowling changed the spell's name.

Reparo

PRONUNCIATION *Reh-pair-oh*

USE To fix a broken object

ETYMOLOGY In Latin, *reparo* means "repair."

PREFERRED WAND MOVEMENT

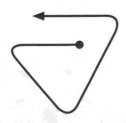

MAGIC MOMENT In *Deathly Hallows*, Harry is able to use the Elder Wand to repair his broken wand with this spell—usually this spell would not be able to fix a snapped wand's magical abilities.

NOTES This spell should not be used to heal humans or animals.

will result in severe scarring.

Repello Inimicum

PRONUNCIATION
Ruh-pell-oh in-ih-mee-kum

USE To repel enemies

ETYMOLOGY In Latin, *repello* means "repel" and *inimīcus* means "enemy."

MAGIC MOMENT In the film *Deathly Hallows: Part 2*, Filius Flitwick casts this charm as a protective enchantment on Hogwarts.

NOTES This spell is also mentioned in the *LEGO Harry Potter: Years 5–7* video game.

Repello Muggletum

PRONUNCIATION Ruh-pell-oh mug-gull-tum

USE To keep Muggles away from an area

ETYMOLOGY In Latin, *repello* means "repel."

MAGIC MOMENT The grounds for the Quidditch World Cup had Muggle-Repelling Charms "on every inch of it." If a Muggle came near, they would suddenly remember something important they had to do and immediately leave.

NOTES According to *Fantastic Beasts and Where to Find Them*, this charm is also used to protect the habitats of certain magical creatures.

Restoring Spell

PRONUNCIATION Unknown

USE To restore an Animagus to his or her human form

ETYMOLOGY N/A

MAGIC MOMENT In *Prisoner of Azkaban,* Sirius Black and Remus Lupin use this spell to prove Ron's pet rat Scabbers is actually Peter Pettigrew.

> **NOTES** When cast, this spell produces a bright blue-white light.

Rictusempra

PRONUNCIATION *Rick-tuh-sem-prah*

USE To make the target weaken with laughter

ETYMOLOGY In Latin, *rictus* means "gaping mouth" and *sempra* means "always."

PREFERRED WAND MOVEMENT

MAGIC MOMENT In *Chamber of Secrets,* Harry casts this spell on Draco Malfoy during the first meeting of the Dueling Club.

> **NOTES** In the *Chamber of Secrets* film, this spell has the effect of throwing Draco across the room instead of making him laugh.

Riddikulus

PRONUNCIATION *Ri-dik-you-lus*

USE To turn a Boggart into something funny

ETYMOLOGY In Latin, *ridiculum* means "joke."

MAGIC MOMENT In *Prisoner of Azkaban*, third-year students needed to climb into a trunk and defeat a Boggart with this spell as part of their end-of-year exams.

NOTES Technically this spell on its own does not banish a Boggart—it is the caster's laughter that does this.

Rowboat Spell

PRONUNCIATION Unknown

USE To propel a rowboat without oars

ETYMOLOGY N/A

MAGIC MOMENT In *Sorcerer's Stone*, Rubeus Hagrid uses this spell to ferry first-years across the Great Lake to Hogwarts.

NOTES This may be the same spell Hagrid used when collecting Harry from the Hut-on-the-Rock.

Salvio Hexia

PRONUNCIATION *Sal-vee-oh hex-ee-ah*

USE To deflect hexes

ETYMOLOGY In Latin, *salvia* means "without breaking" and *hexia* means "hexes."

MAGIC MOMENT In *Deathly Hallows*, Hermione regularly casts this spell to protect herself, Harry and Ron from being detected by Death Eaters.

NOTES This spell is also referenced in the video game *Hogwarts Mystery*.

Scourgify

PRONUNCIATION *Skur-jih-fy*

USE To clean an object

ETYMOLOGY Likely from English *scour*, meaning "to clean."

PREFERRED WAND MOVEMENT

MAGIC MOMENT In *Goblet of Fire*, Hermione teaches this charm to Neville Longbottom so he can clean frog guts from under his fingernails.

NOTES Also known as a Scouring Charm. According to *Fantastic Beasts and Where to Find Them*, Scouring Charms are necessary to get rid of a Bundimun infestation.

Silencio

PRONUNCIATION *Sih-len-see-oh*

USE To silence a target

ETYMOLOGY In Latin, *silencio* means "silence."

MAGIC MOMENT In *Order of the Phoenix*, Filius Flitwick has fifth-year students practice this charm on ravens and bullfrogs.

NOTES According to *Fantastic Beasts and Where to Find Them*, Fwoopers are magical birds that must be sold with Silencing Charms on them, as their song will drive any listeners insane. Those who own the colorful birds must recast this charm monthly.

Skurge

PRONUNCIATION *Skurj*

USE To clear away ectoplasms and frighten spirits

ETYMOLOGY Likely from English *scourge*, meaning "affliction" as a noun and "punish" as a verb.

MAGIC MOMENT Filius Flitwick teaches this spell to second-year students in the *Chamber of Secrets* video game.

NOTES In *The Standard Book of Spells (Grade 2)*, Miranda Goshawk recommends using this charm instead of relying on a can of Mrs. Scower's Magic Mess Remover.

Sonorus

PRONUNCIATION *So-nohr-us*

USE To make a sound louder

ETYMOLOGY In Latin, *sonorus* means "loud."

MAGIC MOMENT In *Goblet of Fire*, Ludo Bagman uses this charm on his own voice so he can commentate during the Quidditch World Cup.

NOTES This may have also been the spell Molly Weasley used in *Half-Blood Prince* to turn up the radio while Fleur Delacour was complaining.

Specialis Revelio

PRONUNCIATION *Spe-see-ah-lis reh-vel-ee-oh*

USE To identify the ingredients in a potion or the enchantment on an object

ETYMOLOGY In Latin, this is a phrase that means "reveal the particulars."

MAGIC MOMENT In *Half-Blood Prince*, Hermione uses this spell on a vial of poison during Potions class so she could brew an antidote.

NOTES Horace Slughorn also refers to this charm as "Scarpin's Revelaspell."

Spongify

PRONUNCIATION *Spun-jih-fy*

USE To soften a target

ETYMOLOGY Likely from English *sponge.*

PREFERRED MOVEMENT

MAGIC MOMENT In the *Sorcerer's Stone* video game, Filius Flitwick teaches this spell to first-year students.

> **NOTES** This spell mostly appears in the *Harry Potter* video games and *Trading Card Game.*

Stupefy

PRONUNCIATION *Stoo-pih-fy*

USE To make a target unconscious

ETYMOLOGY In Latin, *stupeo* means "stunned."

PREFERRED MOVEMENT

MAGIC MOMENT In *Order of the Phoenix,* Minerva McGonagall is hit in the chest with several Stunning Spells while attempting to defend Rubeus Hagrid, who was being evicted by Dolores Umbridge and several Aurors. Her recovery required a stay at St. Mungo's Hospital.

> **NOTES** This spell is not equally effective on all creatures/beings. For example, many dragon keepers must cast this spell together to Stupefy a dragon.

Or Hagrid, part giant.

Supersensory Charm

PRONUNCIATION Unknown

USE To sense things outside of the caster's normal range

ETYMOLOGY N/A

MAGIC MOMENT In *Deathly Hallows*, Ron says he can use a Supersensory Charm instead of rearview mirrors while driving a car.

NOTES It is unclear for how long this charm lasts, or if it only enhances certain senses.

Tergeo

PRONUNCIATION *Tur-gee-oh*

USE To clean up a target

ETYMOLOGY In Latin, *tergere* means "to wipe off."

MAGIC MOMENT In *Half-Blood Prince*, Hermione uses this spell to clean blood from Harry's face after Draco Malfoy had broken his nose.

NOTES This may be related to the Scouring Charm.

Trace Charm

PRONUNCIATION Unknown

USE To detect magical activity done by (or near) underage witches and wizards

ETYMOLOGY N/A

MAGIC MOMENT In *Deathly Hallows*, the Order of the Phoenix plans to move Harry from 4 Privet Drive via broomstick because the Trace would have alerted the Death Eaters to their movements.

NOTES The Trace is automatically lifted when a witch or wizard becomes 17 years old.

Unbreakable Charm

PRONUNCIATION Unknown

USE To make an object unbreakable

ETYMOLOGY N/A

MAGIC MOMENT In *Goblet of Fire*, Hermione places Rita Skeeter, who is in beetle form, inside a jar with an Unbreakable Charm on it to prevent her from escaping.

NOTES This is the only time this charm is mentioned throughout the series.

Undetectable Extension Charm

PRONUNCIATION *Capacious Extremis*

USE To increase the interior dimensions of an object while maintaining its exterior dimensions

ETYMOLOGY In Latin, *capax* means "able to take in" and *in extremis* means "to the limit."

MAGIC MOMENT In *Chamber of Secrets*, Arthur Weasley illegally used this charm on a Ford Anglia so it could fit himself, Molly, Percy, Fred, George, Ron and Ginny Weasley, plus Harry and all of their school supplies.

NOTES According to J.K. Rowling, Hogwarts school trunks are issued with these charms. This spell's incantation was not mentioned in the books or movies but was later revealed on Pottermore.

Waddiwasi

PRONUNCIATION *Wah-dee-wah-see*

USE To send a soft mass to a certain place

ETYMOLOGY In Swedish, *vadd* means "a soft mass" and in French, *vas-y* means "go there."

MAGIC MOMENT In *Prisoner of Azkaban*, Remus Lupin uses this charm to remove the wad of chewing gum Peeves had placed in a keyhole and send it up Peeves's nose.

NOTES It is likely other nouns could be combined with the "wasi" portion of this charm.

Washing Up Spell

PRONUNCIATION Unknown

USE To make dishes wash themselves

ETYMOLOGY N/A

MAGIC MOMENT In *Chamber of Secrets*, Molly Weasley nonverbally uses this spell after making breakfast for Harry.

> **NOTES** This is a type of household magic.

Wingardium Leviosa

PRONUNCIATION
Win-gar-dee-um lev-ee-oh-sa

USE To make a target levitate

ETYMOLOGY In Latin, *wing* and *arduus* mean "high" or "steep" and *levo* means "levitate."

PREFERRED WAND MOVEMENT

MAGIC MOMENT In *Sorcerer's Stone*, Ron uses this spell to make a troll's club levitate, then knocks out the troll by letting the club fall on its head.

> **NOTES** According to the *Book of Spells*, the mass able to be lifted and the amount of time it stays in the air is contingent on the skill of the caster.

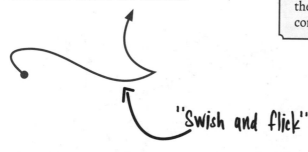

"Swish and flick"

Generally speaking:
jinxes are annoying, hexes
are a little more serious
and curses are the Darkest
forms of magic.

✳ CHAPTER 3 ✳

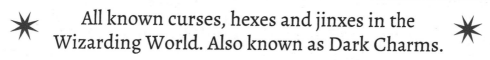

CURSES, HEXES & JINXES

All known curses, hexes and jinxes in the
Wizarding World. Also known as Dark Charms.

Anteoculatia

TYPE Hex

PRONUNCIATION Ann-tee-oh-coo-lay-she-ah

USE To make a target's hair become antlers

ETYMOLOGY In Spanish, the noun *ante* means "buckskin." *Oculus* is Latin for "eyes."

MAGIC MOMENT In *Order of the Phoenix*, Pansy Parkinson is hit with this spell during the student rebellion that occurs after the Weasley twins make their escape from Hogwarts.

NOTES Gilbert Wimple may have been experimenting with this spell shortly before the Quidditch World Cup in *Goblet of Fire*, as he showed up with horns coming out of his head.

Anti-Disapparition Jinx

TYPE Jinx

PRONUNCIATION Unknown

USE To prevent witches and wizards from Disapparating from a set area

ETYMOLOGY N/A

MAGIC MOMENT Albus Dumbledore uses this spell to prevent Death Eaters from leaving the Ministry of Magic after the Battle of the Department of Mysteries in *Order of the Phoenix*.

NOTES This jinx is what prevents anyone from disapparating from Hogwarts.

Doesn't work on house-elves.

Avada Kedavra

TYPE Curse

PRONUNCIATION *Ah-vah-da kuh-dahv-ra*

USE To kill

ETYMOLOGY According to an interview J.K. Rowling gave at the 2004 Edinburgh Book Festival, "It is an ancient spell in Aramaic, and it is the original of *abracadabra*, which means 'let the thing be destroyed.' Originally, it was used to cure illness and the 'thing' was the illness, but I decided to make it the 'thing' as in the person standing in front of me. I take a lot of liberties with things like that. I twist them round and make them mine."

MAGIC MOMENT In the film *Deathly Hallows: Part 2*, Bellatrix Lestrange attempts to use this spell to kill Ginny Weasley, who deflects it with a Shield Charm. In the books, Ginny dodges the spell, as it had been established that Avada Kedavra cannot be deflected with any charms. In both versions, Bellatrix's attempt on Ginny's life enrages Molly Weasley, who then kills Lestrange in a duel.

NOTES Also known as the Killing Curse, Avada Kedavra is one of the three Unforgivable Curses, and its use in the Wizarding World has been outlawed. Harry Potter is the only known person to have survived a direct hit from the curse and did so twice: first, as a baby protected by the magic of his mother's love through her sacrifice; and second, as the Master of Death—by having possessed the Elder Wand, Resurrection Stone and Cloak of Invisibility. In accepting the inevitability of death, he was able to decide to return to the world of the living.

Babbling Curse

TYPE Curse

PRONUNCIATION Unknown

USE To make a target babble whenever they try to speak, presumably

ETYMOLOGY N/A

MAGIC MOMENT In *Chamber of Secrets*, Gilderoy Lockhart alleges that he cured a Transylvanian villager under this curse.

NOTES As the only mention of this curse stems from Gilderoy Lockhart, who is known to exaggerate and lie, it is possible the curse was not cured by him or does not actually exist at all.

Bat-Bogey Hex

TYPE Hex

PRONUNCIATION Unknown

USE To turn a target's bogeys into bats that fly out of their nose

ETYMOLOGY N/A

MAGIC MOMENT In *Half-Blood Prince*, Horace Slughorn asked Ginny Weasley to join the "Slug Club" after seeing her cast this hex on Zacharias Smith.

NOTES This spell was invented by Miranda Goshawk.

Bedazzling Hex

TYPE Hex

PRONUNCIATION Unknown

USE To temporarily blind a target, presumably

ETYMOLOGY N/A

MAGIC MOMENT In *Deathly Hallows*, Xenophilius Lovegood states that a regular cloak can be enchanted with a Bedazzling Hex so it can be used as an invisibility cloak.

NOTES To bedazzle means to temporarily blind someone with flashes of light.

Brachiabindo

TYPE Unknown

PRONUNCIATION *Bra-kee-ah-bin-do*

USE To bind one's opponent with ropes

ETYMOLOGY In Latin, *bracchium* means "arm" and in Old English, *bindo* means "bind."

MAGIC MOMENT In *Cursed Child*, Cedric Diggory uses this Dark Charm on Delphi in the maze of the Triwizard Tournament.

NOTES This spell can be countered with Emancipare.

Calvario

TYPE Curse

PRONUNCIATION *Kal-var-ee-oh*

USE To remove the target's hair or headdress

ETYMOLOGY In Latin, *calvus* means "bald."

MAGIC MOMENT In *Sorcerer's Stone*, Rubeus Hagrid had to drag Harry away from the book *Curses and Counter-Curses*, which contained this Hair-Loss Curse.

NOTES The incantation for this spell was first mentioned in the *LEGO Harry Potter* video games.

Cantis

TYPE Jinx

PRONUNCIATION *Can-tiss*

USE To make a target sing

ETYMOLOGY In Latin, *cantare* means "to sing."

MAGIC MOMENT The incantation for this jinx is given in the 5-Spell Pack for *LEGO Harry Potter: Years 5–7*.

NOTES This may have been the spell used to enchant the Hogwarts suits of armor, leading them to sing Christmas carols.

Cascading Jinx

TYPE Jinx

PRONUNCIATION Unknown

USE To target multiple enemies

ETYMOLOGY N/A

MAGIC MOMENT This spell is used in the *Deathly Hallows: Part 1* video game.

NOTES This spell works by "exploding" upon being cast and can affect each target within its range.

Colloshoo

TYPE Hex

PRONUNCIATION *Coll-oh-shoo*

USE To make a target's shoes stick to the ground

ETYMOLOGY From the Latin *colligo,* meaning "to bind together," and English *shoe.*

PREFERRED MOVEMENT

MAGIC MOMENT This spell is used in the *Harry Potter Trading Card Game.*

> **NOTES** This is also known as the Stickfast Hex.

Confringo

TYPE Curse

PRONUNCIATION *Con-freen-go*

USE To cause an explosion

ETYMOLOGY In Latin, *confringo* means "smash," "crush" or "ruin."

MAGIC MOMENT In *Deathly Hallows,* Harry uses this curse to destroy the sidecar he had been riding in during the Battle of the Seven Potters.

> **NOTES** According to a Famous Wizard Card, Alberta Toothill used this spell to defeat Samson Wiblin in the 1430 All-England Wizarding Dueling Competition.

Conjunctivitis Curse

TYPE Curse

PRONUNCIATION Unknown

USE To affect the eyes and sight of a target

ETYMOLOGY N/A

MAGIC MOMENT In *Goblet of Fire*, Viktor Krum uses this curse on his dragon in the first task of the Triwizard Tournament. This backfired, as the dragon began convulsing and destroyed some of her own eggs.

NOTES Sirius Black was going to suggest that Harry use this curse in the first task of the Triwizard Tournament, as a dragon's eyes are its weakest point.

Cracker Jinx

TYPE Jinx

PRONUNCIATION Unknown

USE To conjure exploding Wizard Crackers

ETYMOLOGY N/A

MAGIC MOMENT This spell is used in the *Prisoner of Azkaban* video game.

NOTES A Wizard Cracker is very similar in design to Muggle Christmas crackers, except the gifts inside are a bit more peculiar and they go off with a much louder bang.

Wizard crackers also create a cloud of blue smoke.

Crucio

TYPE Curse

PRONUNCIATION *Kroo-see-oh*

USE To cause incredible pain in a target

ETYMOLOGY In Latin, *crucio* means "torture."

MAGIC MOMENT In *Order of the Phoenix*, Harry attempts to use this curse on Bellatrix Lestrange after she kills Sirius Black. It is not very effective; as Bellatrix explains when she taunts Harry, "You need to really want to cause pain."

NOTES As one of the three Unforgivable Curses, punishment for casting this curse on another human being is a life sentence at Azkaban.

Densaugeo

TYPE Hex

PRONUNCIATION *Den-sah-ooh-gee-oh*

USE To elongate a target's teeth

ETYMOLOGY In Latin, *dens* means "tooth" and *augeo* means "increase."

MAGIC MOMENT In *Goblet of Fire*, Hermione was inadvertently hit by this spell while Harry and Draco were dueling in a corridor.

NOTES This spell can be countered with a Shrinking Charm.

Ducklifors

TYPE Jinx

PRONUNCIATION *Duck-lee-fors*

USE To turn a target into a duck

ETYMOLOGY In Latin, *forma* means "shape."

MAGIC MOMENT This spell is used in the *Goblet of Fire* and *LEGO Harry Potter: Years 5–7* video games.

NOTES This spell could also be categorized as a type of transfiguration.

Ear-Shriveling Curse

TYPE Curse

PRONUNCIATION Unknown

USE To make a target's ears shrivel

ETYMOLOGY N/A

MAGIC MOMENT In *Goblet of Fire*, it was mentioned that a pen pal of Bill Weasley's from a Brazilian wizarding school once sent him a hat with this curse on it because Bill could not afford to visit.

NOTES This is the first mention of other wizarding schools in the *Harry Potter* universe.

Ebublio

TYPE Jinx

PRONUNCIATION Ee-bub-lee-oh

USE To trap a target in a large bubble

ETYMOLOGY Likely from the English *bubble*.

MAGIC MOMENT This spell is used in the *Goblet of Fire* video game.

NOTES This jinx is useful for confining Dugbogs and Erklings.

Engorgio Skullus

TYPE Hex

PRONUNCIATION En-gorj-ee-oh skull-us

USE To swell a target's head

ETYMOLOGY From the English *engorge* and *skull*.

MAGIC MOMENT This spell is used in the *LEGO Harry Potter* video games.

NOTES This spell can be countered with Redactum Skullus.

Entomorphis

TYPE Jinx

PRONUNCIATION *En-toe-morf-us*

USE To turn a target into an insect

ETYMOLOGY In Greek, *entomo* means "insect" and *morfi* means "shape."

MAGIC MOMENT This spell is used in the *LEGO Harry Potter* video games.

> **NOTES** This jinx can be purchased at Wiseacre's Wizarding Equipment in Diagon Alley.

they've mislabeled it as a hex, though.

Entrail-Expelling Curse

TYPE Curse

PRONUNCIATION Unknown

USE To expel a target's entrails

ETYMOLOGY N/A

MAGIC MOMENT In *Order of the Phoenix*, it is mentioned that a portrait of Urquhart Rackharrow, who invented this curse, hangs in St. Mungo's Hospital.

> **NOTES** It is unclear why the portrait of an inventor of such a torturous curse would hang in a place of healing.

Expulso

TYPE Curse

PRONUNCIATION *Ecks-pul-so*

USE To cause an explosion

ETYMOLOGY In Latin, *expulso* means "expel."

MAGIC MOMENT In *Deathly Hallows*, Thorfinn Rowle blows up a table with this curse during the fight at the café.

NOTES In the *Deathly Hallows* video games, this spell acts more like an automatic rifle.

Fiendfyre

TYPE Curse

PRONUNCIATION Unknown

USE To create cursed fire

ETYMOLOGY N/A

MAGIC MOMENT In *Deathly Hallows*, Crabbe casts this spell in the Room of Requirement during the Battle of Hogwarts.

NOTES Fiendfyre flames are magical and one of the few ways to destroy a Horcrux. They cannot be extinguished by normal or enchanted water.

Finger-Removing Jinx

TYPE Jinx

PRONUNCIATION Unknown

USE To remove a target's fingers

ETYMOLOGY N/A

MAGIC MOMENT In *Quidditch Through the Ages*, it is mentioned that Goodwin Kneen's wife, Gunhilda, used this jinx on him after he returned home late from a game.

> **NOTES** This jinx can be reversed, as Kneen wrote to his cousin that he "got his fingers back now."

Flagrante

TYPE Curse

PRONUNCIATION *Flah-gran-tay*

USE To make an object burn anyone who touches it

ETYMOLOGY In Latin, *flagrans* means "burning."

MAGIC MOMENT In *Deathly Hallows*, the valuables within the Lestrange vault in Gringotts were protected with both this curse and Gemino.

> **NOTES** In the film version, the valuables are not enchanted with this curse.

Flipendo

TYPE Jinx

PRONUNCIATION *Flee-pen-doh*

USE To knock back an opponent

ETYMOLOGY Likely a pun on the English words *flip* and *end*.

PREFERRED MOVEMENT

MAGIC MOMENT In *Cursed Child*, Draco Malfoy uses this spell while dueling with Harry.

> **NOTES** Also known as a Knockback Jinx. In the video games, Flipendo Duo and Flipendo Tria are more powerful versions of this spell.

Furnunculus

TYPE Curse/Jinx

PRONUNCIATION *Fur-nun-cyoo-lus*

USE To make a person break out in boils or pimples

ETYMOLOGY In English, *furuncle* is another word for a boil.

MAGIC MOMENT In *Goblet of Fire*, Harry jinxes Vincent Crabbe with this spell while George Weasley simultaneously hit him with a Jelly-Legs Jinx. The combination caused small tentacles to sprout on Crabbe's face.

> **NOTES** While George Weasley refers to this spell as the Furnunculus Curse, *Pottermore* describes the same incantation as the Pimple Jinx.

Geminio

TYPE Curse

PRONUNCIATION *Juh-min-ee-oh*

USE To create duplicates of an object

ETYMOLOGY In Latin, *geminare* means "to double."

MAGIC MOMENT In *Deathly Hallows*, the valuables within the Lestrange vault at Gringotts were enchanted with both this and the Flagrante curse. Anything touched inside the vault would multiply endlessly, making it likely any thieves would be crushed.

> **NOTES** According to the *Book of Spells*, Geminio was invented by a pair of reclusive twin witches, Helixa and Syna Hyslop.

Horcrux Curse

TYPE Curse

PRONUNCIATION Unknown

USE To contain a piece of one's soul, preventing death

ETYMOLOGY N/A

Don't know anyone other than Voldemort who would want to exist in an incorporeal form.

MAGIC MOMENT In *Chamber of Secrets*, Harry unknowingly destroys the first Horcrux created by Voldemort, Tom Riddle's diary.

> **NOTES** A Horcrux can only be created after the caster has deliberately committed murder and then casts a spell to separate the damaged portion of their soul and encase it in a separate object or being. As long as the Horcrux remains intact, the caster can never be truly killed, though they may lose their body and need to exist in another form.

Hurling Hex

TYPE Hex

PRONUNCIATION Unknown

USE To make a broomstick attempt to unseat its rider

ETYMOLOGY N/A

MAGIC MOMENT In *Prisoner of Azkaban*, Minerva McGonagall confiscates the Firebolt that was sent anonymously to Harry on the grounds that it might have been enchanted with a Hurling Hex, among other curses.

NOTES This may have been the same hex Quirinus Quirrell used on Harry's broom during a Quidditch match in *Sorcerer's Stone*.

Impedimenta

TYPE Jinx

PRONUNCIATION *Im-ped-uh-men-tah*

USE To slow a target's movement

ETYMOLOGY In Latin, *impedimentum* means "a hindrance."

PREFERRED MOVEMENT

MAGIC MOMENT In *Goblet of Fire*, Harry learns this jinx while preparing for the third task of the Triwizard Tournament. It proves useful on both an Acromantula and a Blast-Ended Skrewt.

NOTES This jinx has also been used to push a target backward or levitate it.

Imperio

TYPE Curse

PRONUNCIATION Im-peer-ee-oh

USE To control a target's actions

ETYMOLOGY In Latin, *imperio* means "to rule."

MAGIC MOMENT In *Half-Blood Prince*, Draco Malfoy uses the Imperius Curse on Madam Rosmerta as part of his plot to murder Albus Dumbledore.

NOTES Imperio is one of the three Unforgivable Curses. Unlike the other two, the target of this curse can resist its effects if they are strong-willed enough. Many people were victim to this curse in both Wizarding Wars.

Puts victims in calm, trance-like state.

Locomotor Wibbly

TYPE Curse

PRONUNCIATION *Loh-koh-moh-tor wib-blee*

USE To make a target's legs collapse

ETYMOLOGY In Latin, *loco* means "place" and *moto* means "moving." Wibbly is likely a reference to the English *wobbly*.

PREFERRED MOVEMENT

MAGIC MOMENT This curse's incantation is given in Vindictus Viridian's *Curses and Counter-Curses*.

NOTES This is also known as the Jelly-Legs Curse/Jinx.

Jelly-Brain Jinx

TYPE Jinx

PRONUNCIATION Unknown

USE To affect a target's mental processes (presumably)

ETYMOLOGY N/A

MAGIC MOMENT In a *Daily Prophet* newsletter, it was reported that many Harpy supporters used this jinx in the riot that took place after a 1999 Puddlemere/Holyhead game.

NOTES Four real-world editions of *The Daily Prophet*, created by J.K. Rowling, were made available to British citizens of the Official *Harry Potter* Fan Club in 1998 and 1999.

Jelly-Fingers Curse

TYPE Curse

PRONUNCIATION Unknown

USE To make a target's fingers become jelly-like

ETYMOLOGY N/A

MAGIC MOMENT In a *Daily Prophet* newsletter, coverage of a Quidditch match between the Pride of Portree and the Appleby Arrows mentioned that the losing team's Seeker accused the winning team's Seeker of casting this curse on him.

NOTES This is the only time this spell is mentioned in the *Harry Potter* universe.

Knee-Reversal Hex

TYPE Hex

PRONUNCIATION Unknown

USE To switch a target's knees from back to front

ETYMOLOGY N/A

MAGIC MOMENT In *Quidditch Through the Ages*, it's mentioned that a woman named Gertie Keddle cast this on a man who came to retrieve his ball from her garden while playing an early form of Quidditch in the 1100s.

NOTES According to *Pottermore*, the Seeker for the Canadian National Team woke up having been hexed with this spell in 1877.

Langlock

TYPE Jinx

PRONUNCIATION *Lang-lock*

USE To make a target's tongue stick to the roof of their mouth

ETYMOLOGY In Latin, *lingua* means "tongue" or "language."

MAGIC MOMENT In *Half-Blood Prince*, Harry uses this spell on Peeves. It stopped the poltergeist from speaking, but he was still able to make rude gestures as he left the room.

NOTES This spell was invented by Severus Snape in the 1970s.

Leek Jinx

TYPE Jinx

PRONUNCIATION Unknown

USE To make leeks sprout from a target's ears

ETYMOLOGY N/A

MAGIC MOMENT In *Prisoner of Azkaban*, a Gryffindor fourth-year and Slytherin sixth-year both went to the hospital wing with leeks coming out of their ears after the students had been scuffling prior to a Quidditch match between their respective houses.

NOTES This is the only time this jinx is mentioned in the *Harry Potter* universe.

Levicorpus

TYPE Jinx

PRONUNCIATION *Lev-ee-kor-puss*

USE To hoist a target in the air by the ankle

ETYMOLOGY In Latin, *levare* means "to lift" and *corpus* means "body."

MAGIC MOMENT In *Order of the Phoenix*, Harry first tests this spell on a sleeping Ron.

NOTES This spell was invented by Severus Snape and was specifically created to be cast nonverbally.

Locomotor Mortis

TYPE Curse

PRONUNCIATION *Loh-koh-moh-tor more-tiss*

USE To stick a target's legs together

ETYMOLOGY In Latin, *loco* means "place," *moto* means "moving" and *mortis* means "death."

PREFERRED MOVEMENT

MAGIC MOMENT In *Sorcerer's Stone*, Draco Malfoy casts this spell on Neville Longbottom, causing the latter to hop all the way back to Gryffindor Tower.

> **NOTES** This spell is also known as the Leg-Locker Curse.

Melofors

TYPE Jinx

PRONUNCIATION *Mel-oh-fors*

USE To encase a target's head in a pumpkin

ETYMOLOGY From English *melon* and Latin *forma*, meaning "shape."

MAGIC MOMENT In the *LEGO Harry Potter* video games, this spell can be used on Erklings.

> **NOTES** While avoiding arrest in *Order of the Phoenix*, it was rumored that Albus Dumbledore gave Cornelius Fudge a pumpkin for a head.

Mimble Wimble

TYPE Curse

PRONUNCIATION *Mim-bill-whim-bill*

USE To bind a target's tongue

ETYMOLOGY Likely based on mumbling noises.

PREFERRED MOVEMENT

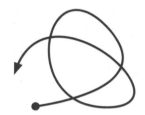

MAGIC MOMENT In the *Chamber of Secrets* video game, Gilderoy Lockhart teaches this spell during Dueling Club.

> **NOTES** In *Sorcerer's Stone*, Vernon Dursley mutters "something that sounded like 'Mimblewimble'" after Hagrid finds out Harry knows nothing of the Wizarding World.

Mucus Ad Nauseam

TYPE Curse

PRONUNCIATION *Myoo-cuss ad naw-see-um*

USE To give a target a strong cold and an extremely runny nose

ETYMOLOGY In Latin, *ad nauseam* means "to the point of nausea."

PREFERRED MOVEMENT

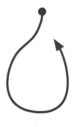

MAGIC MOMENT In *Sorcerer's Stone*, Ron threatens to learn this curse and use it on Hermione and Neville if they caused him and Harry to get caught out of their dorms after-hours to duel Draco Malfoy.

> **NOTES** This curse could likely be countered with a Pepper-Up Potion.

Oppugno

TYPE Jinx

PRONUNCIATION *Oh-pug-no*

USE To attack a target with a specific object or creature

ETYMOLOGY In Latin, *oppugno* means "I assault."

MAGIC MOMENT In *Half-Blood Prince*, Hermione uses this spell to attack Ron with a flock of canaries she had conjured.

NOTES This spell may only work with creatures that are already under the caster's control.

Orbis

TYPE Jinx

PRONUNCIATION *Or-biss*

USE To suck a target into the ground

ETYMOLOGY In Latin, *orbis* means "circle."

MAGIC MOMENT This spell only appears in the *Goblet of Fire* video game.

NOTES This jinx can only be used on a target that's being levitated. The spell's name likely refers to the orb that is created to pull the target down.

Petrificus Totalus

TYPE Curse

PRONUNCIATION *Peh-tri-fih-cus toe-tal-us*

USE To paralyze a target

ETYMOLOGY In Latin, *petrificare* means "to make into stone" and *totalis* means "entire."

PREFERRED MOVEMENT

MAGIC MOMENT In *Half-Blood Prince*, Albus Dumbledore casts this spell on Harry nonverbally to prevent him from moving or speaking during the Battle of the Astronomy Tower. The spell was lifted when Dumbledore died moments later.

> **NOTES** This spell is also referred to as the Full Body-Bind Curse.

Pus-Squirting Hex

TYPE Hex

PRONUNCIATION Unknown

USE To cause yellowish pus to emit from a target's nose

ETYMOLOGY N/A

MAGIC MOMENT In *Half-Blood Prince*, Morfin Gaunt uses this hex on Bob Ogden after he refused to leave the Gaunt property.

> **NOTES** Ogden was able to counter this hex and stop the flow of "nasty yellowish goo" very easily.

Redactum Skullus

TYPE Hex

PRONUNCIATION *Ree-dack-tum skull-us*

USE To shrink a target's head

ETYMOLOGY From the English *redact* and *skull.*

MAGIC MOMENT In *LEGO Harry Potter: Years 1–4,* this spell can be purchased at Wiseacre's Wizarding Equipment.

NOTES This spell can also be used to counter the effects of Engorgio Skullus.

Reducto

TYPE Curse

PRONUNCIATION *Ree-duck-toe*

USE To blast a solid object into a fine mist or ash

ETYMOLOGY In Middle English, *redusen* means "diminish."

PREFERRED WAND MOVEMENT

MAGIC MOMENT In *Goblet of Fire,* Harry uses this spell to blast a hole in the hedge maze during the third task of the Triwizard Tournament.

NOTES This spell is also referred to as the Reductor Curse.

Relashio

TYPE Jinx

PRONUNCIATION *Ree-lash-ee-oh*

USE To release a target's grip on an object

ETYMOLOGY In French, *relâcher* means "to release."

MAGIC MOMENT In *Deathly Hallows*, Hermione forces Corban Yaxley to let go of her by using this jinx.

NOTES This spell is also known as the Revulsion Jinx.

Sardine Hex

TYPE Hex

PRONUNCIATION Unknown

USE To make sardines come out of a target's nose

ETYMOLOGY N/A

MAGIC MOMENT In the *Chamber of Secrets* video game, Rubeus Hagrid comments that he was once hit with a hex that had this effect.

NOTES This may be related to the Slug-Vomiting Charm or the Bat-Bogey Hex.

Sectumsempra

TYPE Curse

PRONUNCIATION *Seck-tum-sem-pra*

USE To deeply cut a target

ETYMOLOGY In Latin, *sectum* means "cut" and *semper* means "always."

MAGIC MOMENT In *Half-Blood Prince*, Harry uses this spell on Draco Malfoy without knowing its effect. It may have killed Draco had Severus Snape not healed him immediately.

NOTES Though cuts caused by this curse can be healed with Vulnera Sanentur, severed body parts cannot be reattached.

that's why George's hearing is all right now.

Slugulus Eructo

TYPE Curse

PRONUNCIATION *Slug-you-luss eh-ruck-toe*

USE To make a target vomit slugs

ETYMOLOGY From the English *slug* and Latin *eructo*, meaning "discharge violently."

MAGIC MOMENT In *Chamber of Secrets*, Ron attempts to use this curse on Draco Malfoy, but his broken wand backfires and causes him to be afflicted instead.

NOTES This spell's incantation is first mentioned in *LEGO Harry Potter: Years 1–4*.

Steleus

TYPE Hex

PRONUNCIATION *Steh-lee-us*

USE To make a target sneeze

ETYMOLOGY In Latin, *stillis* means "drops of liquid."

MAGIC MOMENT This spell is only mentioned in the *Prisoner of Azkaban* video game.

NOTES This spell can be useful for distracting an opponent while dueling.

Stinging Jinx

TYPE Jinx

PRONUNCIATION Unknown

USE To cause severe pain and swelling

ETYMOLOGY N/A

MAGIC MOMENT In *Deathly Hallows*, Hermione uses this spell to disfigure Harry, preventing him from being recognized by the Snatchers.

NOTES It is unclear whether this is the same as a Stinging Hex, which Harry unintentionally used on Severus Snape during an Occlumency lesson.

Taboo

TYPE Jinx

PRONUNCIATION Unknown

USE To set off an alarm when the jinxed word is spoken

ETYMOLOGY N/A

MAGIC MOMENT In *Deathly Hallows*, Death Eaters placed a Taboo on the word "Voldemort." This was effective in catching members of the Order of the Phoenix and the D.A., as others were too fearful to say Lord Voldemort's name.

NOTES Placing a Taboo on a word makes the speaker trackable and breaks any protective enchantments that had been in place.

Tarantallegra

TYPE Jinx

PRONUNCIATION *Tar-ann-tah-lay-grah*

USE To make a target dance uncontrollably

ETYMOLOGY In Italian, the *tarantella* is a certain kind of dance and *allegra* means "happy."

PREFERRED WAND MOVEMENT

MAGIC MOMENT In *Chamber of Secrets*, Draco Malfoy casts this spell on Harry during the first meeting of Dueling Club.

NOTES This spell can work on targets other than humans. In 79 A.D., Warlock Zaccaria Innocenti used this spell to cause a "dance" within Mt. Vesuvius.

Tentaclifors

TYPE Jinx

PRONUNCIATION Ten-tah-clih-fors

USE To turn a target's head into a tentacle

ETYMOLOGY From the English *tentacle* and Latin *forma*, meaning "shape."

MAGIC MOMENT This spell is only mentioned in *LEGO Harry Potter: Years 5–7.*

> **NOTES** It is unclear why this jinx only affects the target's head.

Titillando

TYPE Hex

PRONUNCIATION Tee-tee-lan-doh

USE To tickle and weaken a target

ETYMOLOGY Likely from the English *titillate.*

PREFERRED WAND MOVEMENT

MAGIC MOMENT This spell is listed in Vindictus Viridian's *Curses and Counter-Curses.*

> **NOTES** Also known as the Tickling Hex. It is unclear if or how this spell is different from the Tickling Charm, Rictusempra.

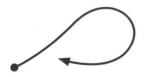

Toenail Growth Hex

TYPE Hex

PRONUNCIATION Unknown

USE To make a target's toenails grow
unusually quickly

ETYMOLOGY N/A

MAGIC MOMENT In *Half-Blood Prince*,
Harry finds this spell in the Prince's copy
of *Advanced Potion-Making* and tests it on
Vincent Crabbe.

NOTES This spell was invented by Severus Snape.

Transmogrifian Torture

TYPE Curse

PRONUNCIATION Unknown

USE To torture a victim until death

ETYMOLOGY N/A

MAGIC MOMENT In *Chamber of Secrets*,
Gilderoy Lockhart incorrectly surmises that
Mrs. Norris had been killed by this curse
when she had actually been petrified.

NOTES *Transmogrify* means "to transform greatly," implying that this curse
may torture targets with grotesque transfigurations.

Trip Jinx

TYPE Jinx

PRONUNCIATION Unknown

USE To make a target trip

ETYMOLOGY N/A

MAGIC MOMENT In *Order of the Phoenix*, Draco Malfoy uses this jinx to capture Harry as he is fleeing the Room of Requirement.

NOTES Targets of this spell feel as though something has caught them around the ankles.

Ventus

TYPE Jinx

PRONUNCIATION *Ven-tuss*

USE To shoot a stream of spiraling wind from the wand

ETYMOLOGY In Latin, *ventus* means "wind."

MAGIC MOMENT This spell is first mentioned in the *Goblet of Fire* video game as a way to attack creatures or objects.

NOTES Ventus Duo and Ventus Tria are more powerful versions of this jinx.

Albus Dumbledore's Forceful Spell

TYPE Spell

PRONUNCIATION Unknown

USE To create great force

ETYMOLOGY N/A

MAGIC MOMENT In *Order of the Phoenix*, Albus Dumbledore uses this spell while battling Voldemort in the Ministry of Magic. It is extremely strong, forcing Voldemort to conjure a shield in order to deflect it.

NOTES Though this spell was strong, it would not have been fatal—Voldemort noted Dumbledore's reluctance to kill him after he deflected the spell.

Antonin Dolohov's Curse

TYPE Curse

PRONUNCIATION Unknown

USE To cause great pain and potentially death

ETYMOLOGY N/A

MAGIC MOMENT During the Battle of the Department of Mysteries in *Order of the Phoenix*, Antonin Dolohov nonverbally inflicts this curse upon Hermione, who immediately collapsed onto the floor. According to Madam Pomfrey, the curse would have done even more damage had Hermione not used a Silencing Charm on Dolohov earlier in the battle.

NOTES This curse produces purple flames that strike the intended target.

Hermione Granger's Jinx

TYPE Jinx

PRONUNCIATION Unknown

USE To cause boils that spell "SNEAK" across the face of a traitor

ETYMOLOGY N/A

MAGIC MOMENT In *Order of the Phoenix*, Hermione enchanted the parchment signed by members of Dumbledore's Army with this spell, though she did not tell any of the signers she had done so. When Marietta Edgecombe tells Dolores Umbridge about the illicit club, it activates the jinx.

NOTES This spell was likely invented by Hermione and was extremely powerful, as neither Madam Pomfrey nor Dolores Umbridge were able to reverse the jinx.

Molly Weasley's Curse

TYPE Curse

PRONUNCIATION Unknown

USE To kill a target

ETYMOLOGY N/A

MAGIC MOMENT During the Battle of Hogwarts, Molly Weasley uses this curse to kill Bellatrix Lestrange, who had enraged her by almost killing Ginny Weasley.

NOTES In the *Deathly Hallows* book, this curse simply kills Bellatrix Lestrange, causing her to fall to the ground. In the film, it causes Lestrange to disintegrate.

Not a complete list.

✳ CHAPTER 4 ✳

ENCHANTED OBJECTS

Remarkable magical objects from
the Wizarding World.

Candy

DESCRIPTION Various sweets and confections

USE To amuse the eater

ENCHANTMENTS Wizarding sweets are commonly made with a wide variety of enchantments and magical ingredients.

Chocolate Frogs are made from 70 percent Croakoa and leap around just as real frogs do.

Bertie Bott's Every-Flavor Beans come in every flavor imaginable.

Drooble's Best Blowing Gum allows the chewer to blow bubbles that won't pop for days and is guaranteed "never to lose its flavor."

Fizzing Whizzbees are sherbet balls that cause a person to levitate while eating them.

Ice Mice cause teeth to "chatter and squeak."

Pepper Imps cause smoke to emit from the ears and nose.

Toothflossing Stringmints floss one's teeth while they are being sucked on.

HISTORY Hogwarts students are able to purchase magical candy from Honeydukes while they are on trips to Hogsmeade. The sweet shop opened in 1641 and is owned by Mr. and Mrs. Ambrosius Flume.

> **NOTES** Any effect from a piece of magical candy is usually temporary and harmless to the consumer.

Fizzing Whizzbees supposedly make you levitate because of dried Billywig stings, not an enchantment.

Cauldrons

DESCRIPTION Large metal cooking pot

USE To facilitate potion-making

ENCHANTMENTS All cauldrons are enchanted to make them lighter to carry. Some cauldrons also have extra enchantments, such as self-stirring cauldrons.

HISTORY According to J.K. Rowling, cauldrons have been in use for centuries.

NOTES Hogwarts first-year students are required to use standard size 2 pewter cauldrons.

Crystal Ball

DESCRIPTION A crystal orb filled with a white smoke

USE To Divine the future

ENCHANTMENTS Unknown

HISTORY The art of looking into crystal balls, also known as orbs, is first taught to Hogwarts students in their third year.

NOTES As evidenced by Sybill Trelawney in the Battle of Hogwarts, crystal balls can also serve well as projectile weapons.

Deathly Hallows

Elder Wand

DESCRIPTION Elder wood, 15 inches, Thestral tail-hair core

USE To perform otherwise impossible feats of magic and defeat all other wands

ENCHANTMENTS N/A

HISTORY According to "The Tale of the Three Brothers," the wand was made by Death and first given to Antioch Peverell. Albus Dumbledore believed the wand was not actually made by Death but by Antioch Peverell himself.

NOTES Also known as the Deathstick or Wand of Destiny.

Resurrection Stone

DESCRIPTION Small stone

USE To return a loved one's spirit from beyond the grave. The stone must be turned three times for this to happen.

ENCHANTMENTS N/A

HISTORY According to "The Tale of the Three Brothers," this stone was made by Death and given to Cadmus Peverell. The stone was passed down from generation to generation and was set in Marvolo Gaunt's ring before Dumbledore hid it in a Snitch for Harry.

NOTES The spirits brought back with the stone are neither ghosts nor flesh and blood.

Cloak of Invisibility

DESCRIPTION A near-perfect invisibility cloak

USE To make the wearer completely invisible to the eye

ENCHANTMENTS N/A

HISTORY According to "The Tale of the Three Brothers," Death gave his own Cloak of Invisibility to Ignotus Peverell. It was then passed down generation by generation, eventually belonging to James Potter, Albus Dumbledore and finally Harry.

NOTES Though the Cloak of Invisibility has remained in perfect condition for generations, it does not protect the wearer from being hit by spells, nor will it prevent the wearer from being seen by other means, such as Alastor Moody's magical eye or spells such as Homenum Revelio.

Owner of all three Hallows becomes the Master of Death.

Deluminator

DESCRIPTION Small silver tube, like a cigarette lighter

USE To remove and replace all lights in an area

ENCHANTMENTS Unknown

HISTORY Invented by Albus Dumbledore, who also enchanted the object to act as a homing device for Ron. In *Deathly Hallows*, it enabled him to hear Harry and Hermione whenever they mentioned his name, then acted as a guide for him to Apparate near them.

NOTES Also known as a Put-Outer.

Floo Powder

DESCRIPTION Glittery powder

USE To allow witches and wizards to travel via fireplaces that are connected to the Floo Network

ENCHANTMENTS Unknown

HISTORY Invented by Ignatia Wildsmith in the 13th century. In Britain, the only producer is Floo-Pow in Diagon Alley.

NOTES Floo Powder has always cost two Sickles per scoop, causing Healer and St. Mungo spokesperson Rutherford Poke to reprimand those who had been injured by using homemade powder for being "cheap."

Seriously, it's a secret.

Flying Carpets

DESCRIPTION A muggle carpet that's enchanted to fly

USE Transportation, especially for small groups

ENCHANTMENTS Flight

HISTORY Flying carpets, or "magic carpets," have long been popular in Asia and the Middle East, though Great Britain has outlawed them due to their status as Muggle Objects.

NOTES Flying carpets were favored as a form of family transportation and are likely much more comfortable than broomsticks.

Foe-Glass

DESCRIPTION A magical mirror

USE To show the enemies of the possessor

ENCHANTMENTS Trace Charm (presumably)

HISTORY Unknown

NOTES This object is a type of Dark Detector. According to Barty Crouch Jr. (posing as Alastor Moody), if he can see the whites of his enemies' eyes, they're right behind him.

Ford Anglia

DESCRIPTION A light blue compact car

USE To transport people and luggage

ENCHANTMENTS Flight, Undetectable Extension Charm, Invisibility

HISTORY Arthur Weasley modified this Muggle car in 1992 or earlier.

NOTES The Ford Anglia inexplicably becomes semi-sentient, as it shows up to save Ron, Harry and Fang from Aragog's family at the end of *Chamber of Secrets*. In Ron's opinion, the Forbidden Forest has made the car wild.

Goblet of Fire

DESCRIPTION A wooden goblet full of blue-white flames

USE To select the champions of the Triwizard Tournament

ENCHANTMENTS Unknown

HISTORY Unknown

NOTES The Goblet is kept in an ancient, jewel-encrusted wooden chest. When it is time to select champions for a new Triwizard Tournament, the box is to be tapped with a wand three times and then opened. A very powerful Confundus Charm is required to make the Goblet break the rules of selection.

Flames turn red when names are selected.

Gubraithian Fire

DESCRIPTION Fire

USE Cooking, warmth, lighting, etc., with no fear of the flames ever going out

ENCHANTMENTS Unknown

HISTORY Albus Dumbledore gifted a branch of this fire to the giants prior to the Second Wizarding War.

NOTES Gubraithian Fire can only be created with a very advanced charm that few wizards are capable of performing.

Hogwarts Portraits

DESCRIPTION Appear as regular paintings that can move

USE Send messages, guard certain areas, give counsel to the current headmaster or headmistress

ENCHANTMENTS Unknown

HISTORY Portraits have long been enchanted by wizarding painters to imitate their visage's general behavior and repeat their favorite phrases. Portraits of the heads of Hogwarts know much more about their subjects due to the heads taking time to teach them before they move on.

NOTES Magical moving photographs can also be made by developing them in a special potion.

Howler

DESCRIPTION A red envelope with a message

USE To play a recorded message in a very loud voice. A Howler will explode if its recipient does not open it quickly.

ENCHANTMENTS Unknown

HISTORY It is unclear when Howlers were first invented, but Neville Longbottom mentioned receiving one from his grandmother prior to Ron receiving one from his mother in 1992. Howlers were also a popular choice for criticizing the Ministry of Magic after the events following the 1994 Quidditch World Cup.

NOTES A Howler's temperature will rapidly increase upon delivery, making it explode if not opened. After its message is played, the letter will burst into flames and leave behind ashes.

Invisibility Cloak

DESCRIPTION An enchanted cloak or one made from Demiguise hair

USE To make the wearer invisible

ENCHANTMENTS Disillusionment Charm or Bedazzling Hex

HISTORY It is unknown when these cloaks began to be manufactured, though Barty Crouch famously hid his son with one after secreting him out of Azkaban.

NOTES Unlike the Cloak of Invisibility, which is a Deathly Hallow, most invisibility cloaks have a shelf life. Demiguise hair will lose its effectiveness over time and charms will slowly wear off.

Knight Bus

DESCRIPTION A purple triple-decker bus

USE To provide magical transport

ENCHANTMENTS Unknown, but likely includes an Imperturbable Charm

HISTORY The Ministry of Magic commissioned the Knight Bus in an effort to provide a means of transportation for the underage and infirm.

> **NOTES** In 1993, it cost 11 Sickles for Harry to travel from Little Whinging to London. Witches or wizards can hail the bus by sticking their wand hand out in the air.

Marauder's Map

DESCRIPTION An enchanted parchment map

USE To plot all of Hogwarts and its grounds and label all the people within its bounds

ENCHANTMENTS Homonculous Charm, Repelling Charm

HISTORY This map was created by James Potter, Sirius Black, Remus Lupin and Peter Pettigrew while they attended Hogwarts. It includes seven secret passageways from Hogwarts to Hogsmeade, though it does not show the Room of Requirement or the Chamber of Secrets.

> **NOTES** The map cannot be tricked by Polyjuice Potion, Animagi or invisibility cloaks. It can only be activated by a person saying, "I solemnly swear that I am up to no good," and will wipe itself again with the phrase, "Mischief managed." A repelling charm of some sort prevents Severus Snape from reading the map and instead causes it to insult him.

Mirror of Erised

DESCRIPTION An ancient mirror with clawed feet and a gold frame. It is inscribed with the phrase "Erised stra ehru oyt ube cafru oyt on wohsi," a mirrored version of "I show not your face but your heart's desire."

USE To show the viewer's deepest desire

ENCHANTMENTS Unknown

HISTORY According to *Pottermore*, no one knows who created the mirror or how it came to reside at Hogwarts.

NOTES In 1991, Albus Dumbledore modified the mirror to become the perfect hiding place for the Sorcerer's Stone. The stone could only be released by a person who wished to find the stone but not use it.

Men have wasted their lives staring at this mirror.

Omnioculars

DESCRIPTION Brass binoculars covered in unusual knobs and dials

USE To zoom, rewind, replay, slow down and overlay words on whatever the user is viewing

ENCHANTMENTS Unknown

HISTORY Omnioculars are known to be sold at Quidditch matches. At the 1994 World Cup, they cost 10 Galleons.

NOTES In Latin, *omni* means "all" and *ocul* means "eye."

Pensieve

DESCRIPTION A shallow stone basin carved with ancient Saxon symbols and runes

USE To review one's memories

ENCHANTMENTS Unknown

HISTORY Pensieves are rare magical items. While personal Pensieves are usually buried with their owners, the Hogwarts Pensieve is passed among heads of the school to serve as a reference source.

NOTES According to Albus Dumbledore, "one simply siphons the excess thoughts from one's mind," puts them in the basin and then reviews them at one's leisure. Pensieves perfectly recreate a moment, allowing the viewer to notice new things.

Probity Probe

DESCRIPTION A thin gold rod, similar to a Muggle security wand

USE To detect concealment spells or hidden magical objects

ENCHANTMENTS Unknown

HISTORY In *Deathly Hallows*, Death Eaters took over Gringotts and were stationed outside its doors with Probity Probes.

NOTES "Probity" refers to the quality of strong moral principles.

Quidditch

Broomsticks

DESCRIPTION An enchanted broomstick

USE To transport witches and wizards. Some models are designed for racing and other games, especially Quidditch.

ENCHANTMENTS Flight (charm unknown), Cushioning Charm, Braking Charm, Disillusionment Charm

HISTORY Earliest known use was in 962, as evidenced by a German manuscript.

NOTES As pointed out in *Quidditch Through the Ages,* wizarding folk were initially very careless with their broomstick use. Muggle depictions of witches and wizards regularly include broomsticks.

Golden Snitch

DESCRIPTION A golden, walnut-sized ball with wings

USE A component in Quidditch. The game ends when a Seeker catches this ball, winning 150 points.

ENCHANTMENTS Flight, Flesh Memory

HISTORY Metal-charmer Bowman Wright invented the Golden Snitch sometime before 1884.

NOTES Since 1269, Seekers traditionally caught small birds called Golden Snidgets. The wizarding community eventually realized the need for a replacement when the birds became endangered.

Bludger

DESCRIPTION A black iron ball, 10 inches in diameter

USE Two Bludgers are present in every Quidditch match. Beaters must keep them away from their own teammates.

ENCHANTMENTS Flight, Bludgeoning

HISTORY The first Bludgers were rocks that had been bewitched to chase players. These proved too easily broken by Beaters' magically reinforced bats, and by the 16th century, iron balls were in use.

NOTES Early Bludgers were known as "Blooders."

Quaffle

DESCRIPTION A red leather ball, about 12 inches in diameter

USE To score points in Quidditch

ENCHANTMENTS Gripping Charm, Anti-Gravity (to fall more slowly)

HISTORY Original Quaffles were made of patched leather and had straps or finger holes. In 1711, the modern red Pennifold Quaffle was developed, and in 1875, Gripping Charms allowed the straps and finger holes to be discontinued.

NOTES In a common foul known as Quaffle-pocking, Chasers alter the Quaffle, usually by poking holes. The goal of this practice is to make the Quaffle zigzag or fall more quickly.

Quills

DESCRIPTION A feather with a pointed tip

USE To write

ENCHANTMENTS Quills may be enchanted with a variety of spells, including:

Anti-Cheating Quills prevent cheating and are required to be used during Hogwarts exams.

Auto-Answer Quills provide answers to questions and are banned from Hogwarts exams.

Spell-Checking Quills correct a user's spelling errors.

Quick-Quotes Quills take notes for their owner (sometimes with great embellishment).

The Black Quill is a Dark object which draws blood from the back of the writer's hand.

The Hogwarts Quill of Acceptance detects the birth of each magical child in the U.K. and Ireland and writes his or her name in the Hogwarts Book of Admittance.

HISTORY Quills have always been the writing implement of choice in the wizarding world, while Muggles switched to more modern pens and pencils.

NOTES Quills can be made from various kinds of feathers, including eagle and pheasant. Gilderoy Lockhart favored a peacock quill for signing autographs. A quill's enchantment is not always permanent; Spell-checking Quills in particular are known for eventually beginning to create more errors than they catch.

Just ask "Roonil Wazlib."

Remembrall

DESCRIPTION A smoke-filled glass ball

USE To remind the owner when something has been forgotten

ENCHANTMENTS Color-Changing Charm

HISTORY In use since at least 1991, as evidenced by Neville Longbottom's possession of one.

NOTES The smoke inside a Remembrall is usually white, but will turn scarlet if held by someone who has forgotten something. Unfortunately, the Remembrall does not tell the holder what has been forgotten.

Revealer

DESCRIPTION A bright red eraser

USE To make invisible ink visible

ENCHANTMENTS Revealing Charm

HISTORY In *Chamber of Secrets*, Hermione attempts to use a Revealer on Tom Riddle's diary.

NOTES Revealers are also mentioned in the *Harry Potter: Hogwarts Mystery* video game.

Secrecy Sensor

DESCRIPTION A Dark Detector shaped like a television antenna

USE To detect lies and concealments

ENCHANTMENTS Unknown

HISTORY Barty Crouch Jr. kept one of these at Hogwarts while posing as Alastor Moody in *Goblet of Fire*.

NOTES The Secrecy Sensor wiggles when lies or concealments are detected. Crouch said it was useless in Hogwarts, where students were always lying, but it would have also been going off constantly due to his own lies.

Sirius Black's Motorcycle

DESCRIPTION A large, magical motorcycle

USE Transportation

ENCHANTMENTS Flight, Enlargement, Dragon's Fire, Net, Brick Wall

HISTORY In 1977, Sirius Black and James Potter used the bike's flying capabilities to evade Muggle police officers who were trying to apprehend them for unknown reasons. The bike was later loaned to Rubeus Hagrid, who used it to transport Harry to the Dursley home. Sixteen years later, Harry leaves 4 Privet Drive in the sidecar of this bike in the Battle of the Seven Potters.

NOTES Sirius left this bicycle to Harry after his death. It was heavily damaged in the Battle of the Seven Potters, but according to J.K. Rowling, Arthur Weasley was eventually able to repair it.

Sneakoscope

DESCRIPTION A Dark Detector that looks like a gyroscope

USE To indicate if someone untrustworthy is nearby by lighting up, whistling and spinning

ENCHANTMENTS Unknown

HISTORY Edgar Stroulger invented this Dark Detector in the 18th century.

NOTES Sneakoscopes vary in expense and sensitivity. Ron purchased a cheap souvenir Sneakoscope while on holiday in Egypt.

Sorcerer's Stone

DESCRIPTION A stone with magical properties

USE To transform any metal into gold and produce the Elixir of Life

ENCHANTMENTS Unknown

HISTORY The only known Sorcerer's Stone was created by Nicolas Flamel, who used it to keep himself and his wife alive for more than six centuries. He and Albus Dumbledore decided to destroy the stone after Voldemort attempted to steal it in 1992.

NOTES Also known as the Philosopher's Stone.

Sorting Hat

DESCRIPTION A very old and dirty pointed wizard's hat

USE To sort first-year students into different Hogwarts houses

ENCHANTMENTS Legilimency

HISTORY The hat originally belonged to Godric Gryffindor, one of the founders of Hogwarts. According to a song the hat sang in 1994, "the founders put some brains in me" so it could continue to choose students for their respective houses after they had passed.

NOTES The hat sings an introductory song before each Sorting Ceremony. According to Nearly-Headless Nick, the hat has been known to warn the school when it senses great danger.

Spellotape

DESCRIPTION Transparent adhesive tape

USE To tape objects together, presumably with magic instead of adhesive

ENCHANTMENTS Sticking Charm (possibly)

HISTORY Spellotape is a very common fix in the magical world and is used to fix or hold together objects where magic would not work or be appropriate. In 1992, Ron kept his broken wand together with Spellotape.

NOTES Spellotape simply holds objects together and does not restore a broken object's magical properties. The name is similar to Sellotape, a British brand of cellophane adhesive tape.

Time-Turner

DESCRIPTION A small gold hourglass, usually worn as a necklace

USE To turn back time in one-hour increments

ENCHANTMENTS Hour-Reversal Charm

HISTORY Time-Turners were recently invented with the help of Professor Saul Croaker, who has studied time-magic in the Department of Mysteries for the entirety of his career. There are hundreds of laws surrounding their use, and they are only to be used to solve extremely trivial matters of time management. By 2020, Theodore Nott had invented a second kind of Time-Turner that allowed the user to travel as far back as they liked and then return to the present.

NOTES According to Croaker, going back more than five hours in time greatly increases the possibility of harming both the traveler and time itself.

Vanishing Cabinet

DESCRIPTION A black and gold cabinet

USE To vanish or transport objects or people

ENCHANTMENTS Vanishing Charm, Transportation Charm

HISTORY According to Arthur Weasley, Vanishing Cabinets were a popular method of escape during the First Wizarding War.

NOTES Vanishing cabinets often come in pairs, but those sold on their own are presumably only used for vanishing unwanted objects.

Weasley Family Clock

DESCRIPTION A clock with nine golden hands

USE To inform the location or status of each person whose name is inscribed on one of the clock's hands

ENCHANTMENTS Trace Charm (presumably)

HISTORY This clock is first mentioned in *Chamber of Secrets*. They do not seem to be common objects, as Molly Weasley does not know anyone else with such a clock.

NOTES The clock lists multiple possible locations, including home, school, work, traveling, lost, hospital, prison or "mortal peril."

Wizard Chess

DESCRIPTION An enchanted chess set with self-moving pieces

USE Game

ENCHANTMENTS Unknown

HISTORY Wizard chess has likely been around for generations. Ron's set used to belong to his grandfather. This is an advantage, as new owners must teach their pieces to trust their judgement.

NOTES With the exception of telling the pieces where to go and the violent fashion in which they take out the opposing pieces, wizard chess is exactly like Muggle chess.

Wizard Wheezes

DESCRIPTION Various games and joke items sold in the wizarding world

USE To amuse the buyer, often as a practical joke

ENCHANTMENTS A wide variety of enchantments are used in making joke products and games.

Canary Creams are sweets that temporarily transform the eater into a canary.

Dungbombs are magical stink bombs invented by Alberic Grunnion in the 1800s.

Exploding Snap is a card game in which the cards explode spontaneously.

Extendable Ears enable a listener to eavesdrop via long flesh-colored pieces of string.

Patented Daydream Charms allow the user to have a highly realistic 30-minute daydream.

Skiving Snackboxes are various types of candies used to induce illness and then cure the ailment, allowing students to feign illness during class.

Ton-Tongue Toffees are enchanted with Engorgement Charms that make the eater's tongue swell.

Weasleys' Wildfire Whiz-Bangs are enchanted fireworks that explode when hit with Stunning Spells and multiply when hit with Vanishing Charms.

HISTORY Hogwarts students often bought these types of goods from Zonko's Joke Shop until it closed during *Half-Blood Prince*, when many shops were suffering as Voldemort rose to power. Around this time, Fred and George Weasley opened Weasleys' Wizard Wheezes in Diagon Alley, where they attracted customers with black humor.

NOTES Many of these items have a long history of being banned from Hogwarts at the insistence of Argus Filch. Despite this, Dungbombs and Skiving Snackboxes were both very popular at Hogwarts, especially during Dolores Umbridge's tenure.

U-No-Poo is scarier than you-know-who.

Media Lab Books
For inquiries, call 646-838-6637

Published by Topix Media Lab
14 Wall Street, Suite 4B
New York, NY 10005

Printed in Canada

ISBN-13: 978-1-948174-24-4
ISBN-10: 1-948174-24-3

MCA-K20-11

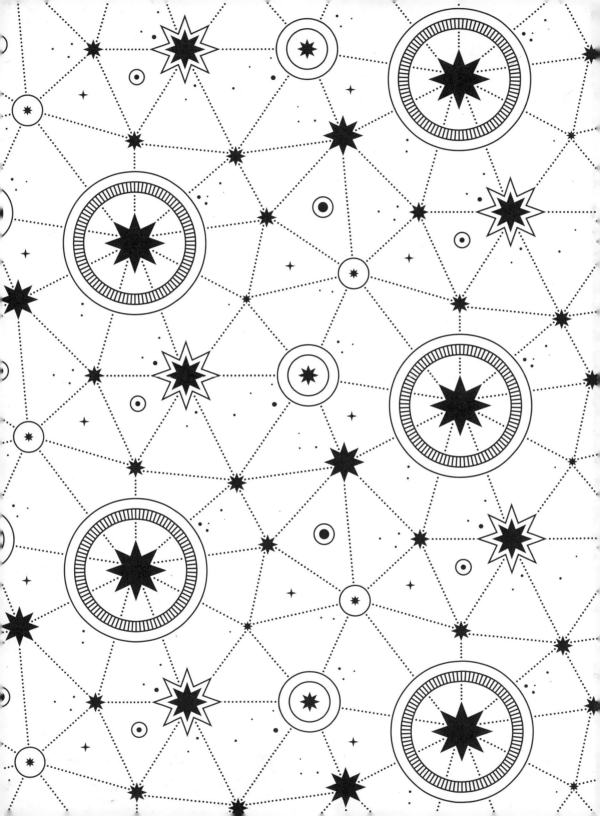